HOW IT IS

Works by Samuel Beckett Published by Grove Press

Cascando and Other Short Dramatic Pieces (Words and Music;
    Eh Joe; Play; Come and Go; Film [original version])
Collected Poems in English & French
The Collected Shorter Plays of Samuel Beckett
The Collected Works of Samuel Beckett [twenty-five volumes]
Company
Disjecta
Endgame
Ends and Odds (Not I; That Time; Footfalls; Ghost Trio; . . . but the
    clouds . . . ; Theatre I; Theatre II; Radio I; Radio II)
Film, A Film Script
First Love and Other Shorts (From an Abandoned Work; Enough,
    Imagination Dead Imagine; Ping; Not I; Breath)
Fizzles
Happy Days
How It Is
I Can't Go On, I'll Go On: A Selection from Samuel Beckett's Work
Ill Seen Ill Said
Krapp's Last Tape and Other Dramatic Pieces (All That Fall; Embers
    [a play for radio]; Act Without Words I and II [mimes])
The Lost Ones
Malone Dies
Mercier and Camier
Molloy
More Pricks Than Kicks
Murphy
Poems in English
Proust
Ohio Impromptu, Catastrophe, and What Where: Three Plays
Rockaby and Other Short Pieces (Ohio Impromptu; All Strange
    Away; A Piece of Monologue)
Stories and Texts for Nothing
Three Novels (Molloy; Malone Dies; The Unnamable)
Waiting for Godot
Watt
Worstward Ho

HOW IT IS

by

Samuel Beckett

Translated from the French
by the author

GROVE PRESS
NEW YORK

Grove Press
841 Broadway
New York, NY 10003

First Evergreen Edition 1964
ISBN: 0-8021-5066-7 (pbk.)
Library of Congress Catalog Card Number: 63-16998

Manufactured in the United States of America

1

how it was I quote before Pim with Pim after Pim how it is
three parts I say it as I hear it

voice once without quaqua on all sides then in me when the
panting stops tell me again finish telling me invocation

past moments old dreams back again or fresh like those that
pass or things things always and memories I say them as I
hear them murmur them in the mud

in me that were without when the panting stops scraps of
an ancient voice in me not mine

my life last state last version ill-said ill-heard ill-recaptured
ill-murmured in the mud brief movements of the lower face
losses everywhere

recorded none the less it's preferable somehow somewhere
as it stands as it comes my life my moments not the millionth
part all lost nearly all someone listening another noting or
the same

here then part one how it was before Pim we follow I quote
the natural order more or less my life last state last version
what remains bits and scraps I hear it my life natural order
more or less I learn it I quote a given moment long past vast
stretch of time on from there that moment and following
not all a selection natural order vast tracts of time

part one before Pim how I got here no question not known
not said and the sack whence the sack and me if it's me no
question impossible too weak no importance

life life the other above in the light said to have been mine on and off no going back up there no question no one asking that of me never there a few images on and off in the mud earth sky a few creatures in the light some still standing

the sack sole good sole possession coal-sack to the feel small or medium five stone six stone wet jute I clutch it it drips in the present but long past long gone vast stretch of time the beginning this life first sign very first of life

then on my elbow I quote I see me prop me up thrust in my arm in the sack we're talking of the sack thrust it in count the tins impossible with one hand keep trying one day it will be possible

empty them out in the mud the tins put them back one by one in the sack impossible too weak fear of loss

no appetite a crumb of tunny then mouldy eat mouldy no need to worry I won't die I'll never die of hunger

the tin broached put back in the sack or kept in the hand it's one or the other I remember when appetite revives or I forget open another it's one or the other something wrong there it's the beginning of my life present formulation

other certainties the mud the dark I recapitulate the sack the tins the mud the dark the silence the solitude nothing else for the moment

I see me on my face close my eyes not the blue the others at the back and see me on my face the mouth opens the tongue comes out lolls in the mud and no question of thirst either no question of dying of thirst either all this time vast stretch of time

life in the light first image some creature or other I watched him after my fashion from afar through my spy-glass sidelong in mirrors through windows at night first image

saying to myself he's better than he was better than yesterday less ugly less stupid less cruel less dirty less old less wretched and you saying to myself and you bad to worse bad to worse steadily

something wrong there

or no worse saying to myself no worse you're no worse and was worse

I pissed and shat another image in my crib never so clean since

I scissored into slender strips the wings of butterflies first one wing then the other sometimes for a change the two abreast never so good since

that's all for the moment there I leave I hear it murmur it to the mud there I leave for the moment life in the light it goes out

on my face in the mud and the dark I see me it's a halt nothing more I'm journeying it's a rest nothing more

questions if I were to lose the tin-opener there's another object or when the sack is empty that family

abject abject ages each heroic seen from the next when will
the last come when was my golden every rat has its heyday
I say it as I hear it

knees drawn up back bent in a hoop I clasp the sack to my
belly I see me now on my side I clutch it the sack we're talking of the sack with one hand behind my back I slip it under
my head without letting it go I never let it go

something wrong there

not fear I quote of losing it something else not known not
said when it's empty I'll put my head in it then my shoulders
my crown will touch the bottom

another image so soon again a woman looks up looks at me
the images come at the beginning part one they will cease
I say it as I hear it murmur it in the mud the images part
one how it was before Pim I see them in the mud a light
goes on they will cease a woman I see her in the mud

she sits aloof ten yards fifteen yards she looks up looks at me
says at last to herself all is well he is working

my head where is my head it rests on the table my hand
trembles on the table she sees I am not sleeping the wind
blows tempestuous the little clouds drive before it the table
glides from light to darkness darkness to light

that's not all she stoops to her work again the needle stops
in midstitch she straightens up and looks at me again she
has only to call me by my name get up come and feel me
but no

I don't move her anxiety grows she suddenly leaves the house and runs to friends

that's all it wasn't a dream I didn't dream that nor a memory I haven't been given memories this time it was an image the kind I see sometimes see in the mud part one sometimes saw

with the gesture of one dealing cards and also to be observed among certain sowers of seed I throw away the empty tins they fall without a sound

fall if I may believe those I sometimes find on my way and then make haste to throw away again

warmth of primeval mud impenetrable dark

suddenly like all that was not then is I go not because of the shit and vomit something else not known not said whence preparatives sudden series subject object subject object quick succession and away

take the cord from the sack there's another object tie the neck of the sack hang it from my neck knowing I'll need both hands or else instinct it's one or the other and away right leg right arm push pull ten yards fifteen yards halt

in the sack then up to now the tins the opener the cord but the wish for something else no that doesn't seem to have been given to me this time the image of other things with me there in the mud the dark in the sack within reach no that doesn't seem to have been put in my life this time useful things a cloth to wipe me that family or beautiful to the feel

which having sought in vain among the tins now one now another in obedience to the wish the image of the moment which when weary of seeking thus I could promise myself to seek again a little later when less weary a little less or try and banish from my thoughts saying true true think no more about it

no the wish to be less wretched a little less the wish for a little beauty no when the panting stops I hear nothing of the kind that's not how I'm told this time

nor callers in my life this time no wish for callers hastening from all sides all sorts to talk to me about themselves life too and death as though nothing had happened me perhaps too in the end to help me last then goodbye till we meet again each back the way he came

all sorts old men how they had dandled me on their knees little bundle of swaddle and lace then followed in my career

others knowing nothing of my beginnings save what they could glean by hearsay or in public records nothing of my beginnings in life

others who had always known me here in my last place they talk to me of themselves of me perhaps too in the end of fleeting joys and of sorrows of empires that are born and die as though nothing had happened others finally who do not know me yet they pass with heavy tread murmuring to themselves they have sought refuge in a desert place to be alone at last and vent their sorrows unheard

if they see me I am a monster of the solitudes he sees man for the first time and does not flee before him explorers bring home his skin among their trophies

suddenly afar the step the voice nothing then suddenly something something then suddenly nothing suddenly afar the silence

life then without callers present formulation no callers this time no stories but mine no silence but the silence I must break when I can bear it no more it's with that I have to last

question if other inhabitants here with me yes or no obviously all-important most important and thereupon long wrangle so minute that moments when yes to be feared till finally conclusion no me sole elect the panting stops and that is all I hear barely hear the question the answer barely audible if other inhabitants besides me here with me for good in the dark the mud long wrangle all lost and finally conclusion no me sole elect

and yet a dream I am given a dream like someone having tasted of love of a little woman within my reach and dreaming too it's in the dream too of a little man within hers I have that in my life this time sometimes part one as I journey

or failing kindred meat a llama emergency dream an alpaca
llama the history I knew my God the natural

she would not come to me I would go to her huddle in her
fleece but they add no a beast here no the soul is de rigueur
the mind too a minimum of each otherwise too great an
honour

I turn to the hand that is free draw it to my face it's a
resource when all fails images dreams sleep food for thought
something wrong there

when the great needs fail the need to move on the need
to shit and vomit and the other great needs all my great
categories of being

then to my hand that is free rather than some other part I
say it as I hear it brief movements of the lower face with
murmur to the mud

it comes close to my eyes I don't see it I close my eyes
something is lacking whereas normally closed or open my
eyes

if that is not enough I flutter it my hand we're talking of my
hand ten seconds fifteen seconds close my eyes a curtain
falls

if that is not enough I lay it on my face it covers it entirely
but I don't like to touch myself they haven't left me that
this time

I call it it doesn't come I can't live without it I call it
with all my strength it's not strong enough I grow mor-

[14]

tal again

my memory obviously the panting stops and question of my memory obviously that too all-important too most important this voice is truly changeable of which so little left in me bits and scraps barely audible when the panting stops so little so faint not the millionth part I say it as I hear it murmur it to the mud every word always

what about it my memory we're talking of my memory not much that it's getting better that it's getting worse that things are coming back to me nothing is coming back to me but to conclude from that

to conclude from that that no one will ever come again and shine his light on me and nothing ever again of other days other nights no

next another image yet another so soon again the third perhaps they'll soon cease it's me all of me and my mother's face I see it from below it's like nothing I ever saw

we are on a veranda smothered in verbena the scented sun dapples the red tiles yes I assure you

the huge head hatted with birds and flowers is bowed down over my curls the eyes burn with severe love I offer her mine pale upcast to the sky whence cometh our help and which I know perhaps even then with time shall pass away

in a word bolt upright on a cushion on my knees whelmed in a nightshirt I pray according to her instructions that's not all she closes her eyes and drones a snatch of the so-called Apostles' Creed I steal a look at her lips

she stops her eyes burn down on me again I cast up mine in haste and repeat awry

the air thrills with the hum of insects

that's all it goes out like a lamp blown out

the space of a moment the passing moment that's all my past little rat at my heels the rest false

false that old time part one how it was before Pim vast stretch of time when I drag myself and drag myself astonished to be able the cord sawing my neck the sack jolting at my side one hand flung forward towards the wall the ditch that never come something wrong there

and Pim part two what I did to him what he said to me

false like that dead head the hand alive still the little table tossing in the clouds the woman jumping to her feet and rushing out into the wind

no matter I don't say any more I quote on is it me is it me I'm not like that any more they have taken that away from me this time all I say is how last how last

part one before Pim before the discovery of Pim have done with that leaving only part two with Pim how it was then leaving only part three after Pim how it was then how it is vast tracts of time my sack sole variable my days my nights my seasons and my feasts it says Lent everlasting then of a sudden Hallowmas no summer that year if it is the same not much real spring my sack thanks to my sack that I keep dying in a dying age

my tins all sorts dwindling but not so fast as appetite different shapes no preference but the fingers know no sooner fastened at random

dwindling in what strange wise but what is strange here undiminished for years then of a sudden half as many

these words of those for whom and under whom and all about the earth turns and all turns these words here again days nights years seasons that family

the fingers deceived the mouth resigned to an olive and given a cherry but no preference no searching not even for a language meet for me meet for here no more searching

the sack when it's empty my sack a possession this word faintly hissing brief void and finally apposition anomaly anomaly a sack here my sack when it's empty bah I've lashings of time centuries of time

centuries I can see me quite tiny the same as now more or less only tinier quite tiny no more objects no more food and I live the air sustains me the mud I live on

the sack again other connexions I take it in my arms talk to it put my head in it rub my cheek on it lay my lips on it turn my back on it turn to it again clasp it to me again say to it thou thou

[17]

say say part one no sound the syllables move my lips and all around all the lower that helps me understand

that's the speech I've been given part one before Pim question do I use it freely it's not said or I don't hear it's one or the other all I hear is that a witness I'd need a witness

he lives bent over me that's the life he has been given all my visible surface bathing in the light of his lamps when I go he follows me bent in two

his aid sits a little aloof he announces brief movements of the lower face the aid enters it in his ledger

my hand won't come words won't come no word not even soundless I'm in need of a word of my hand dire need I can't they won't that too

deterioration of the sense of humour fewer tears too that too they are failing too and there another image yet another a boy sitting on a bed in the dark or a small old man I can't see with his head be it young or be it old his head in his hands I appropriate that heart

question am I happy in the present still such ancient things a little happy on and off part one before Pim brief void and barely audible no no I would feel it and brief apostil barely audible not made not really for happiness unhappiness peace of mind

rats no no rats this time I've sickened them what else at this period part one before Pim vast stretch of time

[18]

the hand dips clawing for the take instead of the familiar slime an arse on his belly he too before that what else that's enough I'm going

not the shit not the vomit something else I'm going the sack tied to my neck I'm ready first thing free play for the leg which leg brief void and barely audible the right it's preferable

I turn on my side which side the left it's preferable throw the right hand forward bend the right knee these joints are working the fingers sink the toes sink in the slime these are my holds too strong slime is too strong holds is too strong I say it as I hear it

push pull the leg straightens the arm bends all these joints are working the head arrives alongside the hand flat on the face and rest

the other side left leg left arm push pull the head and upper trunk rise clear reducing friction correspondingly fall back I crawl in an amble ten yards fifteen yards halt

sleep duration of sleep I wake how much nearer the last

a fancy I am given a fancy the panting stops and a breath-clock breath of life head in the bag oxygen for half an hour wake when you choke repeat five times six times that's enough now I know I'm rested my strength restored the day can begin these scraps barely audible of a fantasy

always sleepy little sleep that's how they're trying to tell me this time sucked down spewed up yawning yawning al-

[19]

ways sleepy little sleep

this voice once quaqua then in me when the panting stops part three after Pim not before not with I have journeyed found Pim lost Pim it is over I am in part three after Pim how it was how it is I say it as I hear it natural order more or less bits and scraps in the mud my life murmur it to the mud

I learn it natural order more or less before Pim with Pim vast tracts of time how it was my vanished life then after then now after Pim how it is my life bits and scraps

I say it my life as it comes natural order my lips move I can feel them it comes out in the mud my life what remains ill-said ill-recaptured when the panting stops ill-murmured to the mud in the present all that things so ancient natural order the journey the couple the abandon all that in the present barely audible bits and scraps

I have journeyed found Pim lost Pim it's over that life those periods of that life first second now third pant pant the panting stops and I hear barely audible how I journey with my sack my tins in the dark the mud crawl in an amble towards Pim unwitting bits and scraps in the present things so ancient hear them murmur them as they come barely audible to the mud

part one before Pim the journey it can't last it lasts I'm calm calmer you think you're calm and you're not in the lowest depths and you're on the edge I say it as I hear it and that death death if it ever comes that's all it dies it dies and I see a crocus in a pot in an area in a basement a saffron the sun creeps up the wall a hand keeps it in the sun this yellow flower with a string I see the hand long image hours long the sun goes the pot goes down lights on the ground the hand goes the wall goes

rags of life in the light I hear and don't deny don't believe don't say any more who is speaking that's not said any more it must have ceased to be of interest but words like now before Pim no no that's not said only mine my words mine alone one or two soundless brief movements all the lower no sound when I can that's the difference great confusion

I see all sizes life included if that's mine the light goes on in the mud the prayer the head on the table the crocus the old man in tears the tears behind the hands skies all sorts different sorts on land and sea blue of a sudden gold and green of the earth of a sudden in the mud

but words like now words not mine before Pim no no that's not said that's the difference I hear it between then and now one of the differences among the similarities

the words of Pim his extorted voice he stops I step in all the needful he starts again I could listen to him for ever but mine have done with mine natural order before Pim the little I say no sound the little I see of a life I don't deny don't believe but what believe the sack perhaps the dark the mud death perhaps to wind up with after so much life there are moments

how I got here if it's me no question too weak no interest but here this place where I begin this time present formulation part one my life clutch the sack it drips first sign this place a few scraps

you are there somewhere alive somewhere vast stretch of time then it's over you are there no more alive no more then again you are there again alive again it wasn't over an error you begin again all over more or less in the same place or in another as when another image above in the light you come to in hospital in the dark

the same as which which place it's not said or I don't hear it's one or the other the same more or less more humid fewer gleams no gleam what does that mean that I was once somewhere where there were gleams I say it as I hear it every word always

more humid fewer gleams no gleam and hushed the dear sounds pretext for speculation I must have slipped you are in the depths it's the end you have ceased you slip you continue

another age yet another familiar in spite of its strangenesses this sack this slime the mild air the black dark the coloured images the power to crawl all these strangenesses

but progress properly so called ruins in prospect as in the dear tenth century the dear twentieth that you might say to yourself to a dream greenhorn ah if you had seen it four hundred years ago what upheavals

ah my young friend this sack if you had seen it I could hardly drag it and now look my vertex touches the bottom

and I not a wrinkle not one

at the end of the myriads of hours an hour mine a quarter of an hour there are moments it's because I have suffered must have suffered morally hoped more than once despaired to match your heart bleeds you lose your heart drop by drop weep even an odd tear inward no sound no more images no more journeys no more hunger or thirst the heart is going you'll soon be there I hear it there are moments they are good moments

paradise before the hoping from sleep I come to sleep return between the two there is all all the doing suffering failing bungling achieving until the mud yawns again that's how they're trying to tell me this time part one before Pim from one sleep to the next

then Pim the lost tins the groping hand the arse the two cries mine mute the birth of hope on with it get it over have it behind me feel the heart going hear it said you're nearly there

be with Pim have been with Pim have him behind me hear it said he'll come back another will come better than Pim he's coming right leg right arm push pull ten yards fifteen yards you stay quiet where you are in the dark the mud and on you suddenly a hand like yours on Pim two cries his mute

you will have a little voice it will be barely audible you will whisper in his ear you will have a little life you will whisper it in his ear it will be different quite different quite a differ-

[23]

ent music you'll see a little like Pim a little life music but in your mouth it will be new to you

then go for good and no goodbyes that age will be over all the ages or merely you no more journeys no more couples no more abandons ever again anywhere hear that

how it was before Pim first say that natural order the same things the same things say them as I hear them murmur them to the mud divide into three a single eternity for the sake of clarity I wake and off I go all life part one before Pim how it was leaving only with Pim how it was leaving only after Pim how it was how it is when the panting stops bits and scraps I wake off I go my day my life part one bits and scraps

asleep I see me asleep on my side or on my face it's one or the other on my side it's preferable which side the right it's preferable the sack under my head or clasped to my belly clasped to my belly the knees drawn up the back bent in a hoop the tiny head near the knees curled round the sack Belacqua fallen over on his side tired of waiting forgotten of the hearts where grace abides asleep

I know not what insect wound round its treasure I come back with empty hands to me to my place what to begin with ask myself that last a moment with that

what to begin my long day my life present formulation last a moment with that coiled round my treasure listening my God to have to murmur that

twenty years a hundred years not a sound and I listen not a gleam and I strain my eyes four hundred times my only sea-

son I clasp the sack closer to me a tin clinks first respite
very first from the silence of this black sap

something wrong there

the mud never cold never dry it doesn't dry on me the air
laden with warm vapour of water or some other liquid I
sniff the air smell nothing a hundred years not a smell I
sniff the air

nothing dries I clutch the sack first real sign of life it drips a
tin clinks my hair never dry no electricity impossible fluff it
up I comb it that can happen there's another object straight
back there's another of my resources was once not now any
more part three there's another difference

the morale at the outset before things got out of hand satis-
factory ah the soul I had in those days the equanimity that's
why they gave me a companion

it's still my day part one before Pim my life present formulation the very beginning bits and scraps I come back to me to
my place in the dark the mud clutch the sack a tin clinks I
make ready I'm going end of the journey

to speak of happiness one hesitates those awful syllables
first asparagus burst abscess but good moments yes I assure
you before Pim with Pim after Pim vast tracts of time good
moments say what I may less good too they must be expected I hear it I murmur it no sooner heard dear scraps
recorded somewhere it's preferable someone listening another noting or the same never a plaint an odd tear inward
no sound a pearl vast tracts of time natural order

suddenly like all that happens to be hanging on by the finger-nails to one's species that of those who laugh too soon alpine image or speluncar atrocious moment it's here words have their utility the mud is mute

here then this ordeal before I go right leg right arm push pull ten yards fifteen yards towards Pim unwitting before that a tin clinks I fall last a moment with that

enough indeed nearly enough when you come to think of it to make you laugh feel yourself falling and hang on with a squeak brief movements of the lower face no sound if you could come to think of it of what you nearly lost and then this splendid mud the panting stops and I hear it barely audible enough to make you laugh soon and late if you could come to think of it

escape hiss it's air of the little that's left of the little whereby man continues standing laughing weeping and speaking his mind nothing physical the health is not in jeopardy a word from me and I am again I strain with open mouth so as not to lose a second a fart fraught with meaning issuing through the mouth no sound in the mud

it comes the word we're talking of words I have some still it would seem at my disposal at this period one is enough aha signifying mamma impossible with open mouth it comes I let it at once or in extremis or between the two there is room to spare aha signifying mamma or some other thing some other sound barely audible signifying some other thing no matter the first to come and restore me to my dignity

passing time is told to me and time past vast tracts of time
the panting stops and scraps of an enormous tale as heard
so murmured to this mud which is told to me natural order
part three it's there I have my life

my life natural order more or less in the present more or less
part one before Pim how it was things so ancient the journey
last stage I come back to me to my place clutch the sack it
drips a tin clinks loss of species one word no sound it's the
beginning of my life present formulation I can go pursue
my life it will still be a man

what to begin with drink to begin with I turn over on my
face that lasts a good moment I last with that a moment in
the end the mouth opens the tongue comes out lolls in the
mud that lasts a good moment they are good moments perhaps the best difficult to choose the face in the mud the
mouth open the mud in the mouth thirst abating humanity
regained

sometimes in this position a fine image fine I mean in movement and colour blue and white of clouds in the wind sometimes some days this time as it happens this day in the mud
a fine image I'll describe it it will be described then go right
leg right arm push pull towards Pim he does not exist

sometimes in this position I fall asleep again the tongue goes
in the mouth closes the mud opens it's I who fall asleep
again stop drinking and sleep again or the tongue out and
drink all night all the time I sleep that's my night present
formulation I have no other I wake from sleep how much
nearer to the last that of men of beasts too I wake ask my-

self how much nearer I quote on last a moment with that
it's another of my resources

the tongue gets clogged with mud that can happen too only
one remedy then pull it in and suck it swallow the mud or
spit it out it's one or the other and question is it nourishing
and vistas last a moment with that

I fill my mouth with it that can happen too it's another of
my resources last a moment with that and question if swal-
lowed would it nourish and opening up of vistas they are
good moments

rosy in the mud the tongue lolls out again what are the
hands at all this time one must always try and see what the
hands are up to well the left as we have seen still clutches
the sack and the right

the right I close my eyes not the blue the others at the
back and finally make it out way off on the right at the end
of its arm full stretch in the axis of the clavicle I say it as I
hear it opening and closing in the mud opening and closing
it's another of my resources it helps me

it can't be far a bare yard it feels far it will go some day on
its four fingers having lost its thumb something wrong there
it will leave me I can see it close my eyes the others and see
it how it throws its four fingers forward like grapnels the
ends sink pull and so with little horizontal hoists it moves
away it's a help to go like that piecemeal it helps me

and the legs and the eyes the blue closed no doubt no since
suddenly another image the last there in the mud I say it as
I hear it I see me

I look to me about sixteen and to crown all glorious weather egg-blue sky and scamper of little clouds I have my back turned to me and the girl too whom I hold who holds me by the hand the arse I have

we are if I may believe the colours that deck the emerald grass if I may believe them we are old dream of flowers and seasons we are in April or in May and certain accessories if I may believe them white rails a grandstand colour of old rose we are on a racecourse in April or in May

heads high we gaze I imagine we have I imagine our eyes open and gaze before us still as statues save only the swinging arms those with hands clasped what else

in my free hand or left an undefinable object and consequently in her right the extremity of a short leash connecting her to an ash-grey dog of fair size askew on its hunkers its head sunk stillness of those hands

question why a leash in this immensity of verdure and emergence little by little of grey and white spots lambs little by little among their dams what else the bluey bulk closing the scene three miles four miles of a mountain of modest elevation our heads overtop the crest

we let go our hands and turn about I dextrogyre she sinistro she transfers the leash to her left hand and I the same instant to my right the object now a little pale grey brick the empty hands mingle the arms swing the dog has not moved I have the impression we are looking at me I pull in my tongue close my mouth and smile

seen full face the girl is less hideous it's not with her I am concerned me pale staring hair red pudding face with pimples protruding belly gaping fly spindle legs sagging knocking at the knees wide astraddle for greater stability feet splayed one hundred and thirty degrees fatuous half-smile to posterior horizon figuring the morn of life green tweeds yellow boots all those colours cowslip or suchlike in the buttonhole

again about turn introrse at ninety degrees fleeting face to face transfer of things mingling of hands swinging of arms stillness of dog the rump I have

suddenly yip left right off we go chins up arms swinging the dog follows head sunk tail on balls no reference to us it had the same notion at the same instant Malebranche less the rosy hue the humanities I had if it stops to piss it will piss without stopping I shout no sound plant her there and run cut your throat

brief black and there we are again on the summit the dog askew on its hunkers in the heather it lowers its snout to its black and pink penis too tired to lick it we on the contrary again about turn introrse fleeting face to face transfer of things swinging of arms silent relishing of sea and isles heads pivoting as one to the city fumes silent location of steeples and towers heads back front as though on an axle

suddenly we are eating sandwiches alternate bites I mine she hers and exchanging endearments my sweet girl I bite she swallows my sweet boy she bites I swallow we don't yet coo with our bills full

my darling girl I bite she swallows my darling boy she bites
I swallow brief black and there we are again dwindling
again across the pastures hand in hand arms swinging heads
high towards the heights smaller and smaller out of sight
first the dog then us the scene is shut of us

some animals still the sheep like granite outcrops a horse
I hadn't seen standing motionless back bent head sunk animals know

blue and white of sky a moment still April morning in the
mud it's over it's done I've had the image the scene is empty
a few animals still then goes out no more blue I stay
there

way off on the right in the mud the hand opens and closes
that helps me it's going let it go I realize I'm still smiling
there's no sense in that now been none for a long time
now

my tongue comes out again lolls in the mud I stay there no
more thirst the tongue goes in the mouth closes it must be a
straight line now it's over it's done I've had the image

that must have lasted a good moment with that I have lasted
a moment they must have been good moments soon it will
be Pim I can't know the words can't come solitude soon over
soon lost those words

I have had company mine because it amuses me I say it as
I hear it and a little girl friend's under the sky of April or of
May we are gone I stay there

way off on the right the tugging hand the mouth shut grim the staring eyes glued to the mud perhaps we shall come back it will be dusk the earth of childhood glimmering again streaks of dying amber in a murk of ashes the earth must have been on fire when I see us we are already at hand

it is dusk we are going tired home I see only the naked parts the solidary faces raised to the east the pale swaying of the mingled hands tired and slow we toil up towards me and vanish

the arms in the middle go through me and part of the bodies shades through a shade the scene is empty in the mud the sky goes out the ashes darken no world left for me now but mine very pretty only not like that it doesn't happen like that

I wait for us perhaps to come back and we don't come back for the evening perhaps to whisper to me what the morning had sung and that day to that morning no evening

find something else to last a little more questions who were they what beings what point of the earth that family whence this dumb show better nothing eat something

that must have lasted a moment there must be worse moments hope blighted is not the worst the day is well advanced eat something that will last a moment they will be good moments

then if necessary my pain which of my many the deep beyond reach it's preferable the problem of my pains the solution last a moment with that then go not because of the shit and vomit something else it's not known not said end of the journey

right leg right arm push pull ten yards fifteen yards arrival new place readaptation prayer to sleep pending which questions if necessary who they were what beings what point of the earth

they will be good moments then less good that too must be expected it will be night present formulation I can sleep and if ever I wake

and if ever mute laugh I wake forthwith catastrophe Pim and end of part one leaving only part two leaving only part three and last

the panting stops I am on my side which side the right it's preferable I part the mouth of the sack and questions what my God can I desire what hunger to eat what was my last meal that family time passes I remain

it's the scene of the sack the two hands part its mouth what can one still desire the left darts in the left hand in the sack it's the scene of the sack and the arm after up to the armpit and then

it strays among the tins without meddling with how many announces a round dozen fastens who knows on the last prawns these details for the sake of something

it brings out the little oval tin transfers it to the other hand goes back to look for the opener finds it at last brings it out the opener we're talking of the opener with its spindle bone handle to the feel rest

the hands what are the hands at when at rest difficult to see with thumb and index respectively pad of tip and outer face of second joint something wrong there nip the sack and with remaining fingers clamp the objects against the palms the tin the opener these details in preference to nothing

a mistake rest we're talking of rest how often suddenly at this stage I say it as I hear it in this position the hands suddenly empty still nipping the sack never let go the sack otherwise suddenly empty

grope in a panic in the mud for the opener that is my life but of what cannot as much be said could not as much be always said my little lost always vast stretch of time

rest then my mistakes are my life the knees draw up the back bends the head comes to rest on the sack between the hands my sack my body all mine all these parts every part

mine say mine to say something to say what I hear in Erebus in the end I'd succeed in seeing my navel the breath is there it wouldn't stir a mayfly's wing I feel the mouth opening

on the muddy belly I saw one blessed day saving the grace of Heraclitus the Obscure at the pitch of heaven's azure towering between its great black still spread wings the snowy body of I know not what frigate-bird the screaming albatross of the southern seas the history I knew my God the natural the good moments I had but last day of the journey it's a good day no surprises good or bad as I went to rest so back I came my hands as I left them I shall lose nothing more see nothing more

the sack my life that I never let go here I let it go needing both hands as when I journey that hangs together ah these sudden blazes in the head as empty and dark as the heart can desire then suddenly like a handful of shavings aflame the spectacle then

need journey when shall I say weak enough later later some day weak as me a voice of my own

with both hands therefore as when I journey or in them take my head took my head above in the light I let go the sack therefore but just a moment it's my life I lie across it therefore that hangs together still

through the jute the edges of the last tins rowel my ribs perished jute upper ribs right side just above where one holds them holds one's sides held one's sides my life that day will not escape me that life not yet

if I was born it was not left-handed the right hand transfers the tin to the other and this to that the same instant the tool pretty movement little swirl of fingers and palms little miracle thanks to which little miracle among so many thanks to which I live on lived on

nothing now but to eat ten twelve episodes open the tin put away the tool raise the tin slowly to the nose irreproachable freshness distant perfume of laurel felicity then dream or not empty the tin or not throw it away or not all that it's not said I can't see no great importance wipe my mouth that without fail so on and at last

take the sack in my arms strain it so light to me lay my cheek on it it's the big scene of the sack it's done I have it behind me the day is well advanced close the eyes at last and wait for my pain that with it I may last a little more and while waiting

prayer in vain to sleep I have no right to it yet I haven't yet deserved it prayer for prayer's sake when all fails when I think of the souls in torment true torment true souls who have no right to it no right ever to sleep we're talking of sleep I prayed for them once if I may believe an old view it has faded

me again always everywhere in the light age unknown seen from behind on my knees arse bare on the summit of a muckheap clad in a sack bottom burst to let the head through holding in my mouth the horizontal staff of a vast banner on which I read

in thy clemency now and then let the great damned sleep here something illegible in the folds then dream perhaps of the good time their naughtiness procured them what time the demons may rest ten seconds fifteen seconds

sleep sole good brief movements of the lower face no sound sole good come quench these two old coals that have nothing more to see and this old kiln destroyed by fire and in all this tenement

all this tenement of naught from top to bottom from hair to toe and finger-nails what little sensation it still has of what it still is in all its parts and dream

dream come of a sky an earth an under-earth where I am inconceivable aah no sound in the rectum a redhot spike that day we prayed no further

how often kneeling how often from behind kneeling from every angle from behind in every posture if he wasn't me he was always the same cold comfort

one buttock twice too big the other twice too small unless an optical illusion here when you shit it's the mud that wipes I haven't touched them for an eternity in other words the ratio four to one I always loved arithmetic it has paid me back in full

Pim's though undersized were iso he could have done with a third I fleshed them indistinctly something wrong there but first have done with my travelling days part one before Pim how it was leaving only part two leaving only part three and last

in the days when I still hugged the walls in the midst of my brotherly likes I hear it and murmur that then above in the light at every bodily pain the moral leaving me as ice I screamed for help with once in a hundred some measure of success

as when exceptionally the worse for drink at the small hour of the garbage-man in my determination to leave the elevator I caught my foot twixt cage and landing and two hours later to the tick someone came running having summoned it in vain

old dream I'm not deceived or I am it all depends on what is not said on the day it all depends on the day farewell rats the ship is sunk a little less is all one begs

a little less of no matter what no matter how no matter when a little less of to be present past future and conditional of to be and not to be come come enough of that on and end part one before Pim

fire in the rectum how surmounted reflections on the passion of pain irresistible departure with preparatives appertaining uneventful journey sudden arrival lights low lights out bye-bye is it a dream

a dream what a hope death of sack arse of Pim end of part one leaving only part two leaving only part three and last Thalia for pity's sake a leaf of thine ivy

quick the head in the sack where saving your reverence I have all the suffering of all the ages I don't give a curse for it and howls of laughter in every cell the tins rattle like castanets and under me convulsed the mud goes guggle-guggle I fart and piss in the same breath

blessed day last of the journey all goes without a hitch the joke dies too old the convulsions die I come back to the open air to serious things had I only the little finger to raise to be wafted straight to Abraham's bosom I'd tell him to stick it up

some reflections none the less while waiting for things to improve on the fragility of euphoria among the different orders of the animal kingdom beginning with the sponges when suddenly I can't stay a second longer this episode is therefore lost the dejections no they are me but I love them the old half-emptied tins let limply fall no something else the mud engulfs all me alone it carries my four stone five stone it yields a little under that then no more I don't flee I am banished

stay for ever in the same place never had any other ambition with my little dead weight in the warm mire scoop my wallow and stir from it no more that old dream back again I live it now at this creeping hour know what it's worth was worth

a great gulp of black air and have done at last with my travelling days before Pim part one how it was before the others the sedentary with Pim after Pim how it was how it is vast tracts of time when I see nothing more hear his voice then this other come from afar on the thirty-two winds from the zenith and depths then in me when the panting stops bits and scraps I murmur them

done with these fidgets that will not brook one second longer here at my ease too weak to raise the little finger and were it the signal for the mud to open under me and then close again

question old question if yes or no this upheaval daily if daily ah to have to hear that word to have to murmur it this upheaval yes or no if daily it so heaves me up and out of my swill

and the day so near its end at last if it is not compact of a thousand days good old question terrible always for the head and universally apropos which is a great beauty to have Pim's timepiece something wrong there and nothing to time I don't eat any more then no I don't drink any more and I don't eat any more don't move any more and don't sleep any more don't see anything any more and don't do anything any more it will come back perhaps all come back or a part I hear yes then no

the voice time the voice it is not mine the silence time the silence that might help me I'll see do something something good God

curse God no sound make mental note of the hour and wait midday midnight curse God or bless him and wait watch in hand but the dark but the days that word again what about them with no memory tear a shred from the sack make knots or the cord too weak

but first have done with my travelling days part one before Pim unspeakable flurry in the mud it's me I say it as I hear it rummaging in the sack taking out the cord tying the neck of the sack tying it to my neck turning over on my face taking leave and away

ten yards fifteen yards semi-side left right leg right arm push pull flat on face imprecations no sound semi-side right left leg left arm push pull flat on face imprecations no sound not an iota to be changed in this description

here confused reckonings to the effect I can't have deviated more than a second or so from the direction imparted to me one day one night at the inconceivable outset by chance by necessity by a little of each it's one of the three from west strong feeling from west to east

and so in the mud the dark on the belly in a straight line as
near as no matter four hundred miles in other words in eight
thousand years if I had not stopped the girdle of the earth
meaning the equivalent

it's not said where on earth I can have received my edu-
cation acquired my notions of mathematics astronomy
and even physics they have marked me that's the main
thing

intent on these horizons I do not feel my fatigue it is mani-
fest none the less passage more laborious from one side to
the other one semi-side prolongation of intermediate pro-
cumbency multiplication of mute imprecations

sudden quasi-certitude that another inch and I fall head-
long into a ravine or dash myself against a wall though
nothing I know only too well to be hoped for in that quarter
this tears me from my reverie I've arrived

the people above whining about not living strange at such
a time such a bubble in the head all dead now others for
whom it is not a life and what follows very strange namely
that I understand them

always understood everything except for example history
and geography understood everything and forgave nothing
never could never disapproved anything really not even
cruelty to animals never loved anything

such a bubble at such a time it bursts the day can't do much
more to me

you mustn't too weak agreed if you want weaker no you must as weak as possible then weaker still I say it as I hear it every word always

my day my day my life so they come back the old words always no not much more only reacclimatize myself then last till sleep not fall asleep mad no sense in that

mad or worse transformed à la Haeckel born in Potsdam where Klopstock too among others lived a space and laboured though buried in Altona the shadow he casts

at evening with his face to the huge sun or his back I forget it's not said the great shadow he casts towards his native east the humanities I had my God and with that flashes of geography

not much more but in the tail the venom I've lost my latin one must be vigilant so a good moment in a daze on my belly then begin I can't believe it to listen

to listen as though having set out the previous evening from Nova Zembla I had just come back to my senses in a subtropical subprefecture that's how I was had become or always was it's one or the other the geography I had

question if always good old question if always like that since the world world for me from the murmurs of my mother shat into the incredible tohu-bohu

like that unable to take a step particularly at night without stopping dead on one leg eyes closed breath caught ears cocked for pursuers and rescuers

I close my eyes the same old two and see me head up rick
in the neck hands tense in the mud something wrong there
breath caught it lasts I last like that a moment until the
quiver of the lower face signifying I am saying have suc-
ceeded in saying something to myself

what can one say to oneself possibly say at such a time a
little pearl of forlorn solace so much the better so much the
worse that style only not so cold cheers alas that style only
not so warm joy and sorrow those two their sum divided
by two and luke like in outer hell

it's soon said once found soon said the lips stiffen and all
the adjacent flesh the hands open the head drops I sink a
little further then no further it's the same kingdom as before
a moment before the same it always was I have never left
it it is boundless

I'm often happy God knows but never more than at this
instant never so oh I know happiness unhappiness I know
I know but there's no harm mentioning it

above if I were above the stars already and from the bel-
freys the brief hour there's not much more left to endure
I'd gladly stay as I am for ever but that won't do

uncord sack and neck I do it I must do it it's the way one
is regulated my fingers do it I feel them

in the mud the dark the face in the mud the hands anyhow
something wrong there the cord in my hand the whole body
anyhow and soon it is as if there at that place and no other
I had lived yes lived always

[43]

God sometimes somewhere at this moment but I have chanced on a good day I would gladly eat something but I won't eat anything the mouth opens the tongue doesn't come out the mouth soon closes again

it's on the left the sack attends me I turn on my right side and take it so light in my arms the knees draw up the back bends the head comes to rest on the sack we must have had these movements before would they were the last

now yes or no a fold of the sack between the lips that can happen not in the mouth between the lips in the vestibule

in spite of the life I've been given I've kept my plump lips two big scarlet blubbers to the feel made for kisses I imagine they pout out a little more part and fasten on a ruck of the sack very horsy

yes or no it's not said I can't see other possibilities pray my prayer to sleep again wait for it to descend open under me calm water at last and in peril more than ever since all parries spent that hangs together still

find more words and they all spent more brief movements of the lower face he would need good eyes the witness if there were a witness good eyes a good lamp he would have them the witness the good eyes the good lamp

to the scribe sitting aloof he'd announce midnight no two in the morning three in the morning Ballast Office brief movements of the lower face no sound it's my words cause them it's they cause my words it's one or the other I'll fall asleep within humanity again just barely

the dust there was then the mingled lime and granite stones piled up to make a wall further on the thorn in flower green and white quickset mingled privet and thorn

the depth of dust there was then the little feet big for their age bare in the dust

the satchel under the arse the back against the wall raise the eyes to the blue wake up in a sweat the white there was then the little clouds you could see the blue through the hot stones through the jersey striped horizontally blue and white

raise the eyes look for faces in the sky animals in the sky fall asleep and there a beautiful youth meet a beautiful youth with golden goatee clad in an alb wake up in a sweat and have met Jesus in a dream

that kind an image not for the eyes made of words not for the ears the day is ended I'm safe till tomorrow the mud opens I depart till tomorrow the head in the sack the arms round it the rest anyhow

brief black long black no knowing and there I am again on my way again something missing here only two or three yards more and then the precipice only two or three last scraps and then the end end of part one leaving only part two leaving only part three and last something missing here things one knows already or will never know it's one or the other

I arrive and fall as the slug falls take the sack in my arms it weighs nothing any more nothing any more to pillow my head I press a rag I shall not say to my heart

no emotion all is lost the bottom burst the wet the dragging the rubbing the hugging the ages old coal-sack five stone six stone that hangs together all gone the tins the opener an opener and no tins I'm spared that this time tins and no opener I won't have had that in my life this time

so many other things too so often imagined never named never could useful necessary beautiful to the feel all I was given present formulation such ancient things all gone but the cord a burst sack a cord I say it as I hear it murmur it to the mud old sack old cord you remain

a little more to last a little more untwine the rope make two ropes tie the bottom of the sack fill it with mud tie the top it will make a good pillow it will be soft in my arms brief movements of the lower face would they were the last

when the last meal the last journey what have I done where been that kind mute screams abandon hope gleam of hope frantic departure the cord round my neck the sack in my mouth a dog

abandoned here effect of hope that hangs together still the eternal straight line effect of the pious wish not to die before my time in the dark the mud not to mention other causes

only one thing to do go back or at least only other thrash round where I lie and I go on zigzag give me my due con-

formably to my complexion present formulation seeking
that which I have lost there where I have never been

dear figures when all fails a few figures to wind up with part
one before Pim the golden age the good moments the losses
of the species I was young I clung on to the species we're
talking of the species the human saying to myself brief
movements no sound two and two twice two and so on

sudden swerve therefore left it's preferable forty-five degrees and two yards straight line such is the force of habit
then right right angle and straight ahead four yards dear
figures then left right angle and beeline four yards then
right right angle so on till Pim

thus north and south of the abandoned arrow effect of hope
series of sawteeth or chevrons sides two yards base three
a little less this the base we're talking of the base in the old
line of march which I thus revisit an instant between two
vertices one yard and a half a little less dear figures golden
age so it ends part one before Pim my travelling days vast
stretch of time I was young all that all those words chevrons
golden vertices every word always as I hear it in me
that was without quaqua on all sides and murmur to
the mud when the panting stops barely audible bits and
scraps

semi-side left right leg right arm push pull flat on face curse
God bless him beseech him no sound with feet and hands
scrabble in the mud what do I hope a tin lost where I have
never been a tin half-emptied thrown away ahead that's all
I hope

where I have never been but others perhaps long before not long before it's one or the other or it's both a procession what comfort in adversity others what comfort

those dragging on in front those dragging on behind whose lot has been whose lot will be what your lot is endless cortège of sacks burst in the interests of all

or a celestial tin miraculous sardines sent down by God at the news of my mishap wherewith to spew him out another week

semi-side right left leg left arm push pull flat on the face mute imprecations scrabble in the mud every half-yard eight times per chevron or three yards of headway clear a little less the hand dips clawing for the take instead of the familiar slime an arse two cries one mute end of part one before Pim that's how it was before Pim

2

here then at last part two where I have still to say how it was as I hear it in me that was without quaqua on all sides bits and scraps how it was with Pim vast stretch of time murmur it in the mud to the mud when the panting stops how it was my life we're talking of my life in the dark the mud with Pim part two leaving only part three and last that's where I have my life where I had it where I'll have it vast tracts of time part three and last in the dark the mud my life murmur it bits and scraps

happy time in its way part two we're talking of part two with Pim how it was good moments good for me we're talking of me for him too we're talking of him too happy too in his way I'll know it later his way of happiness I'll have it later I have not yet had all

faint shrill cry then foretaste of this semi-castrate mutter I must bear how long no more figures there's another little difference compared to what precedes not the slightest figure henceforth all measures vague yes vague impressions of length length of space length of time vague impressions of brevity between the two and hence no more reckoning save possibly algebraical yes I hear yes then no

smartly as from a block of ice or white-hot my hand recoils hangs a moment it's vague in mid air then slowly sinks again and settles firm and even with a touch of ownership already on the miraculous flesh perpendicular to the crack the stump of the thumb and thenar and hypo balls on the left cheek the four fingers on the other the right hand therefore we are not yet head to foot

flat assuredly but slightly arched none the less modesty perhaps the innate kind it can't have been acquired and so a little hog-backed straddling the slit whence contact with the right cheek less pads than nails second cry of fright assuredly but in which I seemed to catch orchestra-drowned a faint flageolet of pleasure already fatuity on my part it's possible

there's a past perhaps this part will work in the past part two with Pim how it was another little difference perhaps compared to what precedes but quick my nails a word on them they will have their part to play

to be feared well well that in this part I may be not extinguished no that is not said that is not yet in my composition no dimmed what is said is dimmed before I flare up Pim gone even more lively if that is possible than before we met more what is the word more lively there's nothing better the man who has only to appear and no ears no eyes for anyone else too strong as always yes to be feared my part now the utility-man's

my part who but for me he would never Pim we're talking of Pim never be but for me anything but a dumb limp lump flat for ever in the mud but I'll quicken him you wait and see and how I can efface myself behind my creature when the fit takes me now my nails

quick a supposition if this so-called mud were nothing more than all our shit yes all if there are not billions of us at the moment and why not the moment there are two there were yes billions of us crawling and shitting in their shit hugging like a treasure in their arms the wherewithal to crawl and shit a little more now my nails my nails well to mention only the hands not to mention that eastern sage they were in a sorry state that extreme eastern sage who having clenched his fists from the tenderest age it's vague till the hour of his death it is not said at what age having done that

the hour of his death at what age it is not said was enabled to see them at last a little before his nails his death having pierced the palms through and through was enabled to see them emerging at last on the other side and a little later having thus lived done this done that clenched his fists all his life thus lived died at last saying to himself latest breath that they'd grow on

the curtains parted part one I saw his friends come to visit him where squatting in the deep shade of a tomb or a bo his fists clenched on his knees he lived thus

they broke for want of chalk or suchlike but not in concert so that some my nails we're talking of my nails some always long others presentable I saw him dreaming the mud parted the light went on I saw him dreaming with the help of a friend or failing that boon all alone of bending them back to the back of his hand for them to go through the other way death forestalled him

Pim's right buttock then first contact he must have heard them grate there's a noble past I could have dug them in if I had wished I longed claw dig deep furrows drink the screams the blue the violent shade the turbaned head bowed over the fists the circle of friends in their white dhotis without going that far

the cries tell me which end the head but I may be mistaken
with the result all hangs together that the hand slides right
and there to be sure there's the fork it's as I thought then
back left just the same just to clinch it and there to be sure
there's the arse again then oh without tarrying down in a
hollow then guided by stump of thumb on spine on up to
the floating ribs that clinches it the anatomy I had no point
in insisting further his cries continue that clinches it this
won't work in the past either I'll never have a past never
had

good a fellow-creature more or less but man woman girl or
boy cries have neither certain cries sex nor age I try to
turn him over on his back no the right side still less the left
less still my strength is ebbing good good I'll never know
Pim but on his belly

all that I say it as I hear it every word always and that
having rummaged in the mud between his legs I bring up
finally what seems to me a testicle or two the anatomy I
had

as I hear it and murmur in the mud that I hoist myself if I
may say so a little forward to feel the skull it's bald no delete
the face it's preferable mass of hairs all white to the feel that
clinches it he's a little old man we're two little old men
something wrong there

in the dark the mud my head against his my side
glued to his my right arm round his shoulders his cries
have ceased we lie thus a good moment they are good
moments

[54]

how long thus without motion or sound of any kind were it but of breath vast a vast stretch of time under my arm now and then a deeper breath heaves him slowly up leaves him at last and sets him slowly down others would say a sigh

thus our life in common we begin it thus I do not say it is not said as others at the end of theirs clinging almost to each other I never saw any it seems never any such but even beasts observe each other I saw some once it seems and they observing each other let him understand who has a wish to I have none

almost clinging that's too strong as always he can't repel me it's like my sack when I had it still this providential flesh I'll never let it go call that constancy if you wish

when I had it still but I have it still it's in my mouth no it's not there any more I don't have it any more I am right I was right

vast stretch of time then for our beginnings a dizzy figure in the days of figures the beginnings of our life in common and question what brings this long peace to a close at last and makes us better acquainted what hitch

a little tune suddenly he sings a little tune suddenly like all that was not then is I listen for a moment they are good moments it can only be he but I may be mistaken

my arm bends therefore my right it's preferable which re-duces from very obtuse to very acute the angle between the humerus and the other the anatomy the geometry and my right hand seeks his lips let us try and see this pretty movement more clearly its conclusion at least

the hand approaches under the mud comes up at a venture
the index encounters the mouth it's vague it's well judged
the thumb the cheek somewhere something wrong there
dimple malar the anatomy all astir lips hairs buccinators it's
as I thought he's singing that clinches it

I can't make out the words the mud muffles or perhaps a
foreign tongue perhaps he's singing a lied in the original
perhaps a foreigner

an oriental my dream he has renounced I too will renounce
I will have no more desires

he can speak then that's the main thing he has the use without having really thought about it I must have thought he
hadn't not having it personally and a little more generally
no doubt that only one way of being where I was namely
my way song quite out of the question I should have
thought

awful moment in any case if there ever was one what vistas
that closes the first phase of our life in common and un-
latches the second and for that matter last more fertile in
vicissitudes and peripeteias the best in my life perhaps best
moment I mean it is difficult to choose

a human voice there within an inch or two my dream perhaps even a human mind if I have to learn Italian obviously
it will be less amusing

but first some remarks very sparsim vast stretch of time
some thirty perhaps in all here are two or three we'll see

oriented as he is he must have been following the same road as I before he dropped there's one

one day we'll set off again together and I saw us the curtains parted an instant something wrong there and I saw us darkly all this before the little tune oh long before helping each other on dropping with one accord and lying biding in each other's arms the time to set off again

to play at him who exists or at least existed then I know I know so much the worse there's no harm in mentioning it no harm is done it does you good now and then they are good moments what does it matter it does no harm to anyone there isn't anyone

there then behind us already at last the first phase of our life in common leaving only the second and last end of part two leaving only part three and last

problem of training and concurrently little by little solution and application of same and concurrently moral plane bud and bloom of relations proper but first some remarks two or three we'll see

moving right my right foot encounters only the familiar mud with the result that while the knee bends to its full extent at the same time it rises my foot we're talking of my foot and rubs down one can see the movement all along Pim's straight stiff legs it's as I thought there's one

my head same movement it encounters his it's as I thought but I may be mistaken with the result it draws back again and launches right the expected shock ensues that clinches it I'm the taller

I resume my pose cleave to him closer he ends at my ankle two or three inches shorter than me I put it down to seniority

now his arms Saint Andrew's cross top V reduced aperture my left hand moves up the left branch follows it into the sack his sack he holds his sack on the inside near the mouth more daring than me my hand lingers a moment on his like cords his veins withdraws and resumes its place on the left in the mud no more about this sack for the moment

in the deeper silence succeeding Pim's song finally vast stretch of time a distant ticking I listen a good moment they are good moments

my right hand sets off along his right arm toils to the limit of its reach and beyond tips with finger-tips a watch wristlet to the feel it's as I thought it will have its part to play yes I hear yes then no

better a big ordinary watch complete with heavy chain he holds it tight in his fist my index worms through the clench-ed fingers and says a big ordinary watch complete with heavy chain

I draw his arm towards me behind his back it jams ticking very greatly improved I drink it for a moment

a few more movements put the arm back where I found it then towards me again the other way overhead sinistro until it jams one can see the movement grasp the wrist with my left hand and pull while bearing from behind with the right on the elbow or thereabouts all that beyond my strength

without having had to raise my head from the mud no
question I finally have the watch to my ear the hand the fist
it's preferable I drink deep of the seconds delicious moments and vistas

released at last the arm recoils sharp a little way then comes
to rest it's I again must put it back where I found it way off
on the right in the mud Pim is like that he will be like that
he stays whatever way he's put but it doesn't amount to
much on the whole a rock

from it to me now part three from way off out on the right
in the mud to me abandoned the distant ticking I derive
no more profit from it none whatever no more pleasure
count no more the unforgiving seconds measure no more
durations and frequencies take my pulse no more ninety
ninety-five

it keeps me company that's all its ticking now and then but
break it throw it away let it run down and stop no something stops me it stops I shake my arm it starts no more
about this watch

no more than I by his own account or my imagination he
had no name any more than I so I gave him one the name
Pim for more commodity more convenience it's off again in
the past

it must have appealed to him it's understandable finished
by appealing to him he was calling him by it himself in the
end long before Pim Pim ad nauseam I Pim I always say
when a man's name is Pim he hasn't the right and all the
things a man hadn't the right always said when his name was
Pim and with that better from that out livelier chattier

[59]

when this has sunk in I let him know that I too Pim my
name Pim there he has more difficulty a moment of confusion irritation it's understandable it's a noble name then
it calms down

me too great benefit too I have that impression great benefit
especially at first hard to say why less anonymous somehow
or other less obscure

me too I feel it forsaking me soon there will be no one
never been anyone of the noble name of Pim yes I hear yes
then no

the one I'm waiting for oh not that I believe in him I say it
as I hear it he can give me another it will be my first Bom he
can call me Bom for more commodity that would appeal
to me m at the end and one syllable the rest indifferent

BOM scored by finger-nail athwart the arse the vowel in
the hole I would say in a scene from my life he would oblige
me to have had a life the Boms sir you don't know the Boms
sir you can shit on a Bom sir you can't humiliate him a Bom
sir the Boms sir

but first have done with this part two with Pim life in common how it was leaving only part three and last when I hear
among other extravagances that he is coming ten yards
fifteen yards who for me for whom I what I for Pim Pim for
me

other extravagances including the use of speech it will
come back to me that much is true it has come back
to me here it is I listen I speak brief movements of the low-

er face with sound in the mud a murmur all sorts one Pim a
life I'm said to have had before him with him after him a
life I'm said to have

training early days or heroic prior to the script the refine-
ments difficult to describe just the broad lines on stop that
family beyond my strength he floundered I floundered but
little by little little by little

between sessions sometimes a sprat a prawn that could
happen it goes on in the past ah if only all past all in the past
Bom come I gone and Bom on our life in common we had
good moments they were good moments drivel drivel no
matter a sprat a prawn

not burst Pim's sack not burst there's no justice or else just
one of those things that pass understanding there are
some

older than mine and not burst perhaps better quality jute
and with that still half-full or else something that escapes
me

sacks that void and burst others never is it possible the old
business of grace in this sewer why want us all alike some
vanish others never

all I hear leave out more leave out all hear no more lie there
in my arms the ancient without end me we're talking of me
without end that buries all mankind to the last cunt they'd
be good moments in the dark the mud hearing nothing
saying nothing capable of nothing nothing

then of a sudden like all that starts starts again no knowing set forth forth again ten yards fifteen yards right leg right arm push pull a few images patches of blue a few words no sound cling to species a few sardines yawn of mud burst the sack drivel on drone on in a word the old road

from the next mortal to the next leading nowhere and saving correction no other goal than the next mortal cleave to him give him a name train him up bloody him all over with Roman capitals gorge on his fables unite for life in stoic love to the last shrimp and a little longer

till the fine day when flip he vanishes leaving me his effects and the sooth comes true the new life no more journeys no more blue a murmur in the mud that's true all must be true and the other on his way ten yards fifteen yards what I for Pim Pim for me

all I hear hear no more lie there the same as before Pim after Pim the same as before in my arms with my sack then of a sudden the old road towards my next mortal ten yards fifteen yards push pull season after season my only season towards my first mortal drivel drivel happily brief

first lesson theme song I dig my nails into his armpit right hand right pit he cries I withdraw them thump with fist on skull his face sinks in the mud his cries cease end of first lesson

second lesson same theme nails in armpit cries thump on skull silence end of second lesson all that beyond my strength

but this man is no fool he must say to himself I would if I
were he what does he require of me or better still what is
required of me that I am tormented thus and the answer
sparsim little by little vast tracts of time

not that I should cry that is evident since when I do I am
punished instanter

sadism pure and simple no since I may not cry

something perhaps beyond my powers assuredly not this
creature is no fool one senses that

what is not beyond my powers known not to be beyond
them song it is required therefore that I sing

what if I were he I would have said it seems to me in the end
to myself but I may be mistaken and God knows I'm not
intelligent otherwise I'd be dead

that or something else the day comes that word again we
come to the day at the end of how long no figures vast
stretch of time when clawed in the armpit long since an
open sore for try a new place one is tempted desperation
more sensitive the eye the glans no only confuse him fatal
thing avoid at all costs

the day then when clawed in the armpit instead of crying
he sings his song the song ascends in the present it's off again
in the present

I withdraw my nails he continues the same air it seems
to me I am rather musical this time I have that in my
life this time and this time on the wing a word or two
eyes skies the or thee cheers we use the same idiom
what a blessing

that's not all he stops nails in armpit he resumes cheers done
it armpit song and this music as sure as if I pressed a button
I can indulge in it any time henceforward

that's not all he continues thump on skull he stops and stop
it likewise the thump on skull signifying stop at all times
and that come to think of it almost mechanically at least
where words involved

why mechanically why simply because it has the effect the
thump on skull we're talking of the thump on skull the effect
of plunging the face in the mud the mouth the nose and
even the eyes and what but words could be involved in the
case of Pim a few words what he can now and then I am not
a monster

I am not going to kill myself demanding something beyond
his powers that he stand on his head for example or on his
feet or kneel most certainly not

or turn over on his back or side no rancour in me any more
no wish any more for anyone to have to do without ceasing
and without ceasing not be able huge cymbals giant arms
outspread two hundred degrees and clang clang miracle
miracle the impossible do the impossible suffer the impossible most certainly not

merely that he sing or speak and not even this rather than that in the early stages merely speak what he will what he can now and then a few words nothing more

first lesson then second series but first take away his sack he resists I claw his left hand to the bone it's not far he cries but won't let go the blood he must have lost by this time vast stretch of time I am not a brute as I may have said before access to the sack that I have my left hand enters gropes for the opener here a parenthesis

no minutiae no problems but all this time we've been together many is the couple would be content with it see each other die without a murmur having had their fill

and Pim all this time vast stretch of time not a movement apart from the lips and thereabouts the lower face to sing cry and convulsive now and again the right hand for pale green the hour to turn that he'll never see and those willy-nilly to be sure by me imparted Pim has not eaten

I yes without its being said all is not said almost nothing and far too much I have eaten offered him to eat crushed against his mouth lost in the hairs the mud my palm dripping with cod's liver or suchlike rubbed it in labour lost if he's still nourished it's on mud if that's what it is I always said so this mud by osmosis long run fulness of time by capillarity

by the tongue when it sticks out the mouth when the lips part the nostrils the eyes when the lids part the anus no it's high and dry the ears no

the urethra perhaps after piss the last drop the blad-
der sucking in a second after all the pumping out
certain pores too the urethra perhaps a certain number
of pores

this mud I always said so it keeps a man going and he clings
to the sack that was the point to be made I say it as I hear
it does it as much as serve to pillow his head no he clutches
it at arm's length as he the window-sill who falls out of
the window

no the truth is this sack I always said so this sack for us here
is something more than a larder than a pillow for the head
than a friend to turn to a thing to embrace a surface
to cover with kisses something far more we don't profit
by it in any way any more and we cling to it I owed
it this tribute

now at rest my left hand part two second half what is it
doing grasping the sack beside Pim's no more about this
sack the opener the opener soon Pim will speak

so many tins still remaining something there that escapes
me I take them out left hand one by one in the mud till at
last the opener put it in my mouth put back the tins I don't
say all and my right arm all this time

all this time vast stretch of time all that beyond my strength
truly with Pim my strength is ebbing it's inevitable we're a
pair my right arm presses him against me love fear of being
abandoned a little of each no knowing not said and
then

then with my right leg thrown crosswise imprison his two one can see the movement take the opener in my right hand move it down along the spine and drive it into the arse not the hole not such a fool the cheek a cheek he cries I withdraw it thump on skull the cries cease it's mechanical end of first lesson second series rest and here parenthesis

this opener where put it when not needed put it back in the sack with the tins certainly not hold it in the hand in the mouth certainly not the muscles relax the mud engulfs where then

between the cheeks of his arse not very elastic but still sufficiently there it's in safety saying to myself I say it as I hear it that with someone to keep me company I would have been a different man more universal

no not there lower down between the thighs it's preferable the point downward and only the little bulb protruding of the piriform handle there it's out of danger saying to myself too late a companion too late

second lesson then second series same principle same procedure third fourth so on vast stretch of time till the day that word again when stabbed in the arse instead of crying he sings his song what a cunt this Pim damn it all confuse arse and armpit horn and steel the thump he gets then I give you my word happily he is no fool he must have said to himself what is required of me now what is the meaning of this new torment

that I should cry no sing no that's the armpit lubricious ferocity no we have seen it is not that really I can't imagine

it is not aimless that is evident this creature is too intelligent to demand what is beyond my powers what then is not beyond my powers to sing to weep what else what else can I do could I do if I were put to the pin of my collar

think perhaps at a pinch it's possible what else am I doing at this moment and bless my soul there it comes again howls thump on skull silence rest

no that's not it either a possible thing no really I can't imagine perhaps I should ask I'll ask some day if I can

no fool merely slow and the day comes we come to the day when stabbed in the arse now an open wound instead of the cry a brief murmur done it at last

with the handle of the opener as with a pestle bang on the right kidney handier than the other from where I lie cry thump on skull silence brief rest jab in arse unintelligible murmur bang on kidney signifying louder once and for all cry thump on skull silence brief rest

so on with now and then lest he get rusty return to the armpit the song ascends that's working thump doused on the spot all this is killing me I'm about to give up when banged on the kidney one day at last he's no fool merely slow instead of crying he articulates hey you me what don't hey you me what don't that's enough I've got it thump on skull done it at last it's not yet second nature but it will be something there that escapes me

I put away the tool between his thighs take my right leg
from off his two imprison his shoulders with my right arm
he can't leave me but I don't trust him long rest saying to
myself the words are there that too late too late indisput-
ably but none the less what an improvement already how
I've improved

orgy of false being life in common brief shames I am not
dead to inexistence not irretrievably time will tell it's telling
but what a hog's wallow pah not even not even pah brief
movements of the lower face profit while ye may silence
gather while ye may deathly silence patience patience

training continued no point skip

table of basic stimuli one sing nails in armpit two speak
blade in arse three stop thump on skull four louder pestle
on kidney

five softer index in anus six bravo clap athwart arse seven
lousy same as three eight encore same as one or two as
may be

all with the right hand I've said this and the left all this time
vast stretch of time it holds the sack I've said this heard it
said now in me that was without quaqua on all sides murmured it in the mud it holds the sack beside Pim's left hand
my thumb has crept between his palm and folded fingers

script and then Pim's voice till he vanishes end of part two
leaving only part three and last

with the nail then of the right index I carve and when it breaks or falls until it grows again with another on Pim's back intact at the outset from left to right and top to bottom as in our civilisation I carve my Roman capitals

arduous beginnings then less he is no fool merely slow in the end he understands all almost all I have nothing to say almost nothing even God that old favourite my rain and shine brief allusions not infrequent as in the tender years it's vague he almost understands

a moment of the tender years the lamb black with the world's sins the world cleansed the three persons yes I assure you and that belief the feeling since then ten eleven that belief said to have been mine the feeling since then vast stretch of time that I'd find it again the blue cloak the pigeon the miracles he understood

that childhood said to have been mine the difficulty of believing in it the feeling rather of having been born octogenarian at the age when one dies in the dark the mud upwards born upwards floating up like the drowned and tattle tattle four full backs of close characters the childhood the belief the blue the miracles all lost never was

the blue there was then the white dust impressions of more recent date pleasant unpleasant and those finally unruffled by emotion things not easy

unbroken no paragraphs no commas not a second for reflection with the nail of the index until it falls and the worn back bleeding passim it was near the end like yesterday vast stretch of time but quick an example from among the simple from the early days or heroic then Pim to speak until he vanishes end of part two leaving only three and last

with the nail then of the right index in great capitals two full lines the shorter the communication the greater the capitals one has only to know a little beforehand what one wants to say he feels the great ornate letter the snakes the imps God be praised it won't be long YOU PIM pause YOU PIM in the furrows here a difficulty has he grasped no knowing

stab him simply in the arse that is to say speak and he will say anything what he can whereas proof I need proof so stab him in a certain way signifying answer once and for all which I do therefore what an improvement how I've improved

a special stroke indescribable a trick of the hand with the gratifying result one fine day vast stretch of time me Jim or Tim not Pim in any case not yet the back is not yet uniformly sensitive but it will be cheers none the less done it more or less rest

simply try again not yet say die a good deep P and the apposite stab and inevitable one fine day should it mean his trying all the consonants in the Roman alphabet that he will answer in the end it's inevitable me Pim which he does in the end it was inevitable me Pim clap athwart the arse opener between the thighs arm round his poor shoulders done it rest

thus then no point in other examples he was a bad pupil I a bad master but fulness of time the little we had to say it was nothing

I nothing only say this say that your life above YOUR LIFE pause my life ABOVE long pause above IN THE in the LIGHT pause light his life above in the light almost an octosyllable come to think of it a coincidence

I then nothing about me my life what life never anything hardly ever he nothing either unless driven never on his own but once launched not without pleasure the impression or illusion no stopping him thump thump all his fat-headed meatus in the shit no holding him thump thump

the proportion of invention vast assuredly vast proportion a thing you don't know the threat the bleeding arse the cracking nerves you invent but real or imaginary no knowing it's impossible it's not said it doesn't matter it does it did that's superb a thing that matters

that life then said to have been his invented remembered a little of each no knowing that thing above he gave it to me I made it mine what I fancied skies especially and the paths he crept along how they changed with the sky and where you were going on the Atlantic in the evening on the ocean going to the isles or coming back the mood of the moment less important the creatures encountered hardly any always the same I picked my fancy good moments nothing left

dear Pim come back from the living he got it from another that dog's life to take and to leave I'll give it to another the voice said so the voice in me that was without quaqua on all sides hard to believe here in the dark the mud that only one life above from age to age eternally allowance made for preferences ah that's it allowance made for needs

mine what I need that's it most need changing aspects that's it ever changing aspects of the never changing life according to the needs but the needs the needs surely for ever here the same needs from age to age the same thirsts the voice says so

it said I murmur for us here one after another the same thirsts and life unchanging here as above according to the unchanging needs hard to believe it depends on the moment the mood of the moment the mood remains a little changeful you may say no sound there is nothing to prevent you today I am perhaps not quite so sad as yesterday there is nothing to stop you

the things I could no longer see little scenes part one in their stead Pim's voice Pim in the light blue of day and blue of night little scenes the curtains parted the mud parted the light went on he saw for me that too may be said there is nothing against it

silence more and more longer and longer silences vast tracts of time we at a loss more and more he for answers I for questions sick of life in the light one question how often no more figures no more time vast figure vast stretch of time on his life in the dark the mud before me mainly curiosity was he still alive YOUR LIFE HERE BEFORE ME utter confusion

God on God desperation utter confusion did he believe he believed then not couldn't any more his reasons both cases my God

I pricked him how I pricked him in the end long before purely curiosity was he still alive thump thump in the mud vile tears of unbutcherable brother

if he heard a voice if only that if he had ever heard a voice voices if only I had asked him that I couldn't I hadn't heard it yet the voice the voices no knowing surely not

I won't either in the end I won't hear it any more never heard it it said so I murmur so no voice only his only Pim's not his either no more Pim never any Pim never any voice hard to believe in the dark the mud no voice no image in the end long before

samples whatever comes remembered imagined no knowing life above life here God in heaven yes or no if he loved me a little if Pim loved me a little yes or no if I loved him a little in the dark the mud in spite of all a little affection find someone at last someone find you at last live together glued together love each other a little love a little without being loved be loved a little without loving answer that leave it vague leave it dark

end of part two part one is ended leaving only part three and last they were good moments there will be good moments less good it must be expected but first a little frisk the last new position and effect on soul

I let go the sack let go Pim that's the worst letting go the
sack and away semi-side left right leg right arm push pull
right right don't lose him round his head hairpin turn right
right straighten up across his arm along his side close in and
halt my head to his feet his to mine long rest growing
anguish

suddenly back hugging the flesh west and north with my
right hand I seize his skin too big for him and pull myself
forward last little frisk back to my place I should never have
left it I'll never leave it again I grasp the sack it has not
stirred Pim has not stirred our hands touch long silence long
rest vast stretch of time

YOUR LIFE ABOVE no more need of light two lines only
and Pim to speak he turns his head tears in the eyes my
tears my eyes if I had any it was then I needed them not
now

his right cheek to the mud his mouth to my ear our narrow
shoulders overlapping his hairs in mine human breath shrill
murmur if too loud finger in arse I'll stir no more from this
place I'm still there

soon unbearable thump on skull long silence vast stretch
of time soon unbearable opener arse or capitals if he
has lost the thread YOUR LIFE CUNT ABOVE
CUNT HERE CUNT as it comes bits and scraps all
sorts not so many and to conclude happy end cut
thrust DO YOU LOVE ME no or nails armpit and
little song to conclude happy end of part two leav-

ing only part three and last the day comes I come to
the day Bom comes YOU BOM me Bom ME BOM you
Bom we Bom

he's coming I'll have a voice no voice in the world but mine
a murmur had a life up above down here I'll see my things
again a little blue in the mud a little white our things little
scenes skies especially and paths

and me see me catch a glimpse ten seconds fifteen seconds
cowering quiet as a mouse in my hole or night come at last
less light a little less hastening towards the next much better much safer that will be good good moments the good
moments I'll have had up there down here nothing left but
go to heaven

samples my life above Pim's life we're talking of Pim my life
up there my wife stop opener arse slow to start then no
holding him thump on skull long silence

my wife above Pam Prim can't remember can't see her she
shaved her mound never saw that I talk like him I do we're
talking of me like him little blurts midget grammar past that
then plof down the hole

I talk like him Bom will talk like me only one kind
of talk here one after another the voice said so it talks
like us the voice of us all quaqua on all sides then in
us when the panting stops bits and scraps that's where
we get it our old talk each his own way each his needs
the best he can it stops ours starts starts again no knowing

Pam Prim we made love every day then every third then the Saturday then just the odd time to get rid of it tried to revive it through the arse too late she fell from the window or jumped broken solumn

in the ward before she went every day all winter she forgave me everybody all mankind she grew good God calling her home the blue mound strange idea not bad she must have been dark on the deathbed it grew again

the flowers on the night-table she couldn't turn her head I see the flowers I held them at arm's length before her eyes the things you see right hand left hand before her eyes that was my visit and she forgiving marguerites from the latin pearl they were all I could find

iron bed glossy white two foot wide all was white high off the ground vision of love in it see others' furniture and not the loved one how can one

sitting on the foot of the bed holding the vase bile-green flute the feet dangling the flowers between the face through them that I forget what it was like except intact white as chalk not a scratch or my eyes roved there were a score of them

outside the road going down lined with trees thousands all the same same species never knew which miles of hill straight as a ribbon never saw that toil in winter to the top the frozen slush the black boughs grey with hoar she at the end at the top dying forgiving all white the holly she had begged for the berries anything a little colour a little green so much white the ivy anything tell her I couldn't find find the words the places she must have done it in summer July August find the words tell her the places where I had looked left foot right foot one step forward two back

my life above what I did in my life above a little of everything tried everything then gave up no worse always a hole a ruin always a crust never any good at anything not made for that farrago too complicated crawl about in corners and sleep all I wanted I got it nothing left but go to heaven

papa no idea building trade perhaps some branch or other fell off the scaffolding on his arse no the scaffolding that fell and he with it landed on his arse dead burst it must have been him or the uncle God knows

mamma none either column of jade bible invisible in the black hand only the edge red gilt the black finger inside psalm one hundred and something oh God man his days as grass flower of the field wind above in the clouds the face ivory pallor muttering lips all the lower it's possible

never anyone never knew anyone always ran fled elsewhere some other place my life above places paths nothing else brief places long paths the quickest way or a thousand detours the safest way always at night less light a little less A to B B to C home at last safe at last drop sleep

first sounds feet whispers clink of iron don't look head in my arms face to the ground macfarlane on top of all turn the head in the cover of the cloak make a chink open the eyes close them quick close the chink wait for night

B to C C to D from hell to home hell to home to hell always
at night Z to A divine forgetting enough

did he think did we think just enough to speak enough to
hear not even comma a mouth an ear sly old pair glued together take away the rest put them in a jar there to end if
it has an end the monologue

dream then that at least certainly not me dream me Pim
Bom to be me think pah

all alone Pim all alone before me his voice come back did he
speak the way I do part three the way I murmur in the mud
what I hear in me when the panting stops bits and scraps if
only I had asked I couldn't I didn't know I didn't speak not
yet he wouldn't have known YES OR NO I don't know I
won't know I didn't ask I won't be asked

my voice is going it will come back my first voice no voice
above none there either Pim's life above never was never
spoke to anyone never solo mute words no sound it's possible brief movements of the lower great confusion no knowing

if Bom never came if only that but then how end the hand
dipping clawing for the tin the arse instead of the familiar
slime all imagination and all the rest this voice its promises
and solaces all imagination dear bud dear worm

all that always every word as I hear it in me that was without when the panting stops and murmur it in the mud bits
and scraps I say it once more every word always I'll
say it no more and now what to end is there anything
left before going on and ending part two leaving on-

ly part three and last yes all alone there is left all alone
alas

all alone and the witness bending over me name Kram bending over us father to son to grandson yes or no and the
scribe name Krim generations of scribes keeping the record
a little aloof sitting standing it's not said yes or no samples
extracts

brief movements of the lower face no sound or too faint

ten yards one hour forty minutes six yards per hour or better
it's clearer one palm per minute I remembered my days
an handbreadth my life as nothing man a vapour

struggles to open tin long struggles couldn't see of what
change our lamps gives up puts back tin and opener in sack
very calm

slept six minutes breathing fitful set off on waking six yards
and an inch or two one hour twelve minutes drops

end of seventh year of stillness beginning of eighth brief
movements of the snout would seem to be eating the mud

three o'clock morning starts muttering my astoundment
then succeed in catching a few scraps Pim Bim proper
names presumably imagination dreams things memories
lives impossible here's my first-born old workshop farewell

monster silences vast tracts of time perfect nothingness reread the ancient's notes pass the time beginning of the murmur his last day lucky devil be in on that what's the use of me

reread our notes pass the time more about me than him hardly a word out of him now not a mum this past year and more I lose the nine-tenths it starts so sudden comes so faint goes so fast ends so soon I'm on it in a flash it's over

no more motion than a slab and forbidden to take our eyes off him what's the use of that Krim says his number's up so is mine we daren't leave him quick all numbers up it's the only solution

yesterday in grandpa's notes the place where he wishes he were dead weakness happily honour of the family shortlived he stuck it out till his time was up whereas happy me tedium inaction don't make me laugh question of character and the business in the blood

I lie by his side happy innovation handier for keeping an eye on him not a quiver that escapes me than squatting on the little stool old style even papa and the state he's in now less the eye than the ear if I may say so it's obvious new methods a necessity

Krim too straight as a die at his stand ballpoint at the ready on the alert for the least never long idle if nothing I invent must keep busy otherwise death

one notebook for the body inodorous farts stools idem pure mud suckings shudders little spasms of left hand in sack quiverings of the lower without sound movements of the head calm unhurried the face raised from the mud or the left cheek or the right cheek and the right cheek or the left cheek laid there in its stead or the face or the right cheek or the left cheek or the face respectively a new development in my opinion a good mark for me what does it remind me of

Kram the Seventh at his last gasp perhaps his face whiter than the pillow-slip and me still a shitty little chit can it be the end at last the long calm agony and me the happy witness elect one notebook for all that in any case entries such as sample eighth of May Victory Day impression that he's sinking Krim says I'm mad

a second for the mutterings verbatim no tampering very little a third this for my comments whereas up till now all pell-mell in the same blue yellow and red respectively simple once you've thought of it

steeping sweating in the light of my lamps he murmurs of darkness can he be blind he must the great blue eyes he opens sometimes and of a companion I see none in his head the dark the friend

forbidden to touch him we might relieve him Krim is all for it and be damned clean his buttocks at least wipe his face what do we risk no one will know you never know safer not

dreamt of the great Kram the Ninth the greatest of us all up to date never met him more's the pity grandpa remembered him raving mad before the limit brought up by force trussed like a faggot Krim vanished never seen again

he the first to have pity happily to no effect honour of the family to eliminate the little stool regrettable innovation discarded and the idea of the three books set aside where's the greatness it is there

rich testimony I agree questionable into the bargain especially the yellow book that is not the voice of here here all self to be abandoned say nothing when nothing

blue the eyes I see them old stone perhaps our new daylight lamps it's possible I agree and in the head the dark and friend I agree but this voice the voice of all what voice I hear none and who all damn it I'm the thirteenth generation

but of course here too no knowing our senses our lights what do they amount to look at me and even if I here thirteen lives I say thirteen but long before who knows how long how many other dynasties

this voice yes the sad truth is there are moments when I fancy I can hear it and my lamps that my lamps are going out Krim says I'm mad

two more years to put in a little more then back to the surface ah no lie down if I could lie down never stir any more I feel I could weakness for pity's sake honour of the family if I could move on a little further if there is a further we on-

ly know this little pool of light there was a time he moved
it's in the book a little further in the mud the dark and
drop my first-born dying to his grandchild your papa's
grandpapa disappeared never came up never seen again
bear it in mind when your time comes

little private book these secret things little book all my own
the heart's outpourings day by day it's forbidden one big
book and everything there Krim imagines I am drawing
what then places faces loved forgotten

that's enough end of extracts yes or no yes or no no no no
witness no scribe all alone and yet I hear it murmur it all
alone in the dark the mud and yet

and now to continue to conclude to be able a few more little
scenes life above in the light as it comes as I hear it word for
word last little scenes I set him off stop him short thump
thump can't take any more or he stops can't give any more
it's one or the other opener instantly or not often not silence
rest

he has stopped I have made him stop suffered him to stop
it's one or the other not specified the thing stops and more
or less long silence not specified more or less long rest I set
him off again opener or capitals as the case may be otherwise never a word new instalment so on

the gaps are the holes otherwise it flows more or less more or
less profound the holes we're talking of the holes not specified not possible no point I feel them and wait till he can
out and on again or I don't and opener or I do and open-

er just the same that helps him out as I hear it as it comes word for word to continue to conclude to be able part two leaving only three and last

what land all lands midnight sun midday night all latitudes all longitudes

all longitudes

what men all colours black to white tried them all then gave up no worse too vague pardon pity home to native land to die in my twenties iron constitution above in the light my life my living made my living tried everything building mostly it was booming all branches plaster mostly met Pam I think

love birth of love increase decrease death efforts to resuscitate through the arse joint vain through the cunt anew vain jumped from window or fell broken column hospital margucrites lies about mistletoe forgiveness

out by day no by night less light a little less hid by day a hole a ruin land strewn with ruins all ages my spinal dog it licked my genitals Skom Skum run over by a dray it hadn't all its wits broken column in my thirties and still alive robust constitution what am I to do

life little scenes just time to see the hangings part heavy swing of black velvet what life whose life ten twelve years old sleeping in the sun at the foot of the wall white dust a palm thick azure little clouds other details silence falls again

what sun what have I said no matter I've said something
that's what was needed seen something called it above said
it was so said it was me ten twelve years old sleeping in the
sun in the dust to have a moment's peace I have it I had it
opener arse following scene and words

sea beneath the moon harbour-mouth after the sun the
moon always light day and night little heap in the stern it's
me all those I see are me all ages the current carries me out
the awaited ebb I'm looking for an isle home at last
drop never move again a little turn at evening to the
sea-shore seawards then back drop sleep wake in the silence
eyes that dare open stay open live old dream on crabs
kelp

astern receding land of brothers dimming lights mountain if
I turn water roughening he falls I fall on my knees crawl
forward clink of chains perhaps it's not me perhaps it's another perhaps it's another voyage confusion with another
what isle what moon you say the thing you see the thoughts
sometimes that go with it it disappears the voice goes on a
few words it can stop it can go on depending on what it's
not known it's not said

on what the nails that can go on the hand dead a fraction of
an inch life a little slow to leave them the hair the head dead
a hoop rolled by a child me higher than him me I fall dis-
appear the hoop rolls on a little way loses way rocks falls
disappears the garden-path is still

can't go on we're talking of me not Pim Pim is finished he
has finished me now part three not Pim my voice not his say-

[86]

ing this these words can't go on and Pim that Pim never was and Bom whose coming I await to finish be finished have finished me too that Bom will never be no Pim no Bom and this voice quaqua of us all never was only one voice my voice never any other

all that not Pim I who murmur all that a voice mine alone and that bending over me noting down one word every three two words every five from age to age yes or no but above all go on impossible for the moment quite impossible that's the essential nay folly I hear it murmur it to the mud folly folly stop your drivel draw the mud about your face children do it in the sand at the sea-shore in the country in the sandpits the humbler

all about pressed tight as a child you would have done it in the sandpits even you the mud above the temples and nothing more be seen but three grey hairs old wig rotting on a muckheap false skull foul with mould and rest you can say nothing when time ends you may end

all that the time it takes to say all that my voice a voice of mine not like that more faint less clear but the purport and back to Pim where abandoned part two it still can end it must end it's preferable only a third to go two fifths then part three leaving only part three

E then good and deep sick of light quick now the end above last thing last sky that fly perhaps gliding on the pane the counterpane all summer before it or noonday glory of colours behind the pane in the mouth of the cave and the approaching veils two veils from left and right they approach come together or one down the other up or aslant diagonal from left or right top corner right or left bottom corner one two three and four they approach come together

a first pair then others on top as many times as necessary or a first one two three or four a second two three four or one a third three four one or two a fourth four one two or three as many times as necessary

for what for to be happy eyes starting pupils staring night in the midst of day better the fly at break of morn four o'clock five o'clock the sun rises its day begins the fly we're talking of a fly its day its summer on the pane the counterpane its life last thing last sky

E then good and deep quick now the end above sick of light and nail on skin for the down-stroke of the Roman N when suddenly too soon too soon a few more little scenes suddenly I cross it out good and deep Saint Andrew of the Black Sea and opener signifying again I'm subject to these whims

my life again above in the light the sack stirs grows still again stirs again the light through the worn thread strains less white sharp sounds distant still but less it's evening he crawls tiny out of the sack me again I'm there again the first is always me then the others

what age my God fifty sixty eighty shrunken kneeling arse on heels hands on ground splayed like feet very clear picture thighs aching the arse rises the head drops touches the straw it's preferable sound of sweeping the dog's tail we want to go on home at last my eyes open still too light I see each halm sounds of hammers three or four at least hammers chisels crosses perhaps or some other ornament

I crawl to the door raise my head yes I assure you peer through a chink and so I would go to the world's end on my knees to the world's end right round it on my knees arms forelegs eyes an inch from the ground I'd smell the world again my laughter in dry weather raises the dust on my knees up the gangways between decks with the emigrants

homer mauve light of evening mauve wave among the streets the serotines abroad already we not yet not such fools I'm the brain of the two sounds distant still but less its the evening air does that one must understand these things and later drawing near that it's only a creaking of wheels drawing near iron felly jolting on the stones the harvest perhaps coming home but the hooves in that case

no matter there I am again how I last on my knees hands joined before my face thumb-tips before my nose finger-tips before the door my crown or vertex against the door one can see the attitude not knowing what to say whom to implore what to implore no matter it's the attitude that counts it's the intention

how I last some day it will be night and all asleep we shall slip out the tail sweeps the straw it hasn't all its wits mine now to think for us both here come the veils most dear from left and right they wipe us away then the rest the whole door away life above little scene I couldn't have imagined it I couldn't thump on skull no point in post mortems and then what then what we'll try and see last words cut thrust a few words DO YOU LOVE ME CUNT no disappearance of Pim end of part two leaving only part three and last one can't go on one goes on as before can one ever stop put a stop that's more like it one can't go on one can't stop put a stop

so Pim stops life above in the light he can't give any more me permitting or thump on skull I can't take any more it's one or the other and what then him me I'll ask him but first me when Pim stops what becomes of me but first the bodies glued together mine on the north good so much for the trunks the legs but the hands when Pim stops where are they the arms the hands what are they at

his right way off on the right axis of the clavicle or cross Saint Andrew of the Volga mine about his shoulders his neck I can't see good so much for the right arms and their hands I can't see it's not said in keeping and the others the left the arms we're talking of our arms full stretch before us the hands together in the sack good so much for the four arms the four hands but how together touching simply or clasped

clasped but how clasped as in the handshake no but his flat mine on top the crooked fingers slipped between his the nails against his palm it's the position they have finally adopted clear picture of that good and parenthesis the vision suddenly too late a little late of how my injunctions by other means more humane my behests by a different set of signals quite different more humane more subtle from left hand to left hand in the sack nails and palm scratching pressing but no always the right hand thump on skull claws in armpit for the song blade in arse pestle on kidney slap athwart and index in hole all the needful up to the end great pity good and the heads

heads together necessarily my right shoulder overriding his left I've the upper everywhere but how together like two old jades harnessed together no but mine my head its face in the mud and his its right cheek in the mud his mouth against my ear our hairs tangled together impression that to separate us one would have to sever them good so much for the bodies the arms the hands the heads

what then became of us him me flop back into the past in this position when the silence when Pim stopped past giving any more me permitting or thump on skull past taking any more I'll ask him but me me

question if what he has said or rather I heard of that voice ruined from such long silence a third two fifths or every word question if there when it stops if somewhere there food for thought prayer without words against a stable-door long icy toil towards the too late all-forgiving what else night at dead water on the deep on the little sea poor in isles or else some other voyage

there wherewith to beguile a moment of this vast season or just a drop of water for the thirst that you drink and goodbye answer just a drop of ditch-water I'd be glad of a sup at this hour

and question what can I ask him now what on earth ask him
further busy myself with that if only a few seconds they
would be good seconds answer no they would not either
question why answer because ah yes there's reason in me
yet because all the things I've asked him and don't as much
as know what but only know if as much that he's there still
half in my arms cleaving to me with all his little length
that's something to know and in that little ageless body
black with mud when the silence falls again enough feeling still for him to be there still

with me someone there with me still and me there still
strange wish when the silence there still enough for me to
wonder if only a few seconds if he is breathing still or in my
arms already a true corpse untorturable henceforward and
this warmth under my arm against my side merely the mud
that stays warm as we have seen words my truant guides
with you strange journeys

merrily then once again push pull if only a herring from
time to time a prawn they would be good moments alas
wrong road we are not on that road any more the tins in the
depths of the sack hermetically under vacuum on their dead
for ever sealed the voice stops for one or the other reason
and life along with it above in the light and we along with
it that is what becomes of us

me at least him I have still to ask what becomes of me at
least when the silence I stop then start again opener or
capitals and in the hairs against my ear the extorted voice
life above a murmur pestle on kidney louder clearer and
what will become of me when I have it no more I'll have an-

other quaqua of us all I didn't say it I didn't know it then
my own I didn't say it

no nothing I said nothing I say it as I hear it I said always
brief movements of the lower no sound Pim's voice in my
ear that I'd have it always and life above not possible otherwise our little scenes blue by day always fine a few fleece
clouds the stars by night heavenly bodies never dark ad
libitum confidential between ourselves secrets a murmur
always and what is more in my opinion I hear it such a
question I murmur it my opinion such a question never
crossed never could my mind such a doubt my opinion I
hear it murmur it never never

in a word Pim's voice then nothing life as we say little scene
one minute two minutes good moments then nothing even
better not a doubt Kram waits one year two years he knows
us something wrong there but all the same two years three
years in the end to Krim they are dead something wrong
there

Krim dead are you mad one doesn't die here and with that
with his long index claw Kram shaken pierces the mud two
little flues to the skins then to Krim right for you they are
warm Krim to Kram roles reversed it's the mud Kram we'll
leave them open and see one year two years Kram's finger
skins still warm

Krim I cannot credit it let us take their temperature Kram
no need the skin is rosy Krim rosy are you mad Kram they
are warm and rosy there it is we are nothing and we are rosy
good moments not a doubt

in a word once more once and for all Pim's voice then nothing nothing then Pim's voice I make it stop suffer it to stop then set it off again that I at last may be no more then at last be again something there that escapes me since how can I opener capitals and not be it's impossible it stands to reason there's reason in me yet

in a word more lively that's what I was getting at I've got at it I say it as I hear it more how shall I say more lively there's nothing better before Pim part one more independent seeing my own little scenes crawling eating thinking even if you insist an odd dim thought losing the one and only opener hanging on to humankind a thousand and one last shifts with emotions laughter even and tears to match soon dried in a word hanging on

nothing too to be sure often nothing in spite of everything dead as mutton warm and rosy always inclined that way ever since the womb if I may judge by what I know less and less that's true of myself since the womb the panting stops I murmur it

even Pim with Pim in the beginning part two first half first quarter more lively when I think that I could as I did train him up as I did conceive that system then apply I can't get over it make it work my undoing for ever since it's clear eyelids part close again quick I've seen myself quite clear ever since nothing left but voice

Pim's then quaqua of us all then mine alone that of us all mine alone after my fashion a murmur in the mud the thin black air nothing left but short waves three hundred four hundred yards per second brief movements of the lower with murmur little tremble flush with the mud one yard two yards me so lively nothing left but words a murmur on and off

so many words so many lost one every three two every five first the sound then the sense same ratio or else not one not one lost I hear all understand all and live again have lived again I don't say above in the light among the shades in search of shade I say here YOUR LIFE HERE in a word my voice otherwise nothing therefore nothing otherwise my voice therefore my voice so many words strung together to the effect first example

to the effect it is leaving me like the others then nothing nothing but nothing then Bom life with Bom the old words back from the dead a few old words his wish he is on my left his right arm about me his left hand in mine in the sack his ear against my mouth my life in the light a murmur a few mouldy old reliables azure that never dies morning with evening in its train other subdivisions of time one or two usual flowers night always too light whatever may be said to the contrary safe places one after another infernal homes he will always have me with him a murmur of moments at will from the long pest that did not finish us then yah solitary rat from head to foot in the dark the mud

and to the effect second example no Pim no Bom I alone my voice no other it leaves me I leave me it comes back to me I come back to me or finally under the lamps third example and last under the ideal observer's lamps sudden flurry of mouth and adjacent all the lower brief dart of rosy tongue a few beads of froth then sudden straight line lips gone no trace of mucus gums clenched arch to arch he suspects nothing but where am I flown then sudden same again then then where do I go from then to then and in between but first quick make an end of life in common end at last of part two leaving only last at last

YOUR LIFE HERE long pause YOUR LIFE HERE good and deep long pause this dead soul what appal I can imagine YOUR LIFE unfinished for murmur light of day light of night little scene HERE to the quick and someone kneeling or huddled in a corner in the gloom start of little scene in the gloom HERE HERE to the bone the nail breaks quick another in the furrows HERE HERE howls thump the whole face in the mud mouth nose no more breath and howls still never saw that before his life here howls in the black air and the mud like an old infant's never to be stifled good try again HERE HERE to the marrow howls to drink solar years no figures until at last good he wins life here this life he can't

questions then DO YOU LOVE ME CUNT that family cut thrust to make an end got there at last if he remembers how he got here no one day he found himself here yes like when one is born yes manner of speaking yes if he knows how long ago no not even a rough idea no if he remembers how he lived no always lived like that yes flat on his belly in the mud yes in the dark yes with his sack yes

never a gleam no never a soul no never a voice no I the first yes never stirred no crawled no a few yards no ate pause ATE good and deep no if he knows what's in the sack no never had the curiosity no if he thinks he can die one day pause DIE ONE DAY no

[96]

never did for anyone what I for him animate no sure yes
never felt another flesh against his no happy no unhappy no
if he feels me against him no only when I torment him
yes

if he likes to sing no but sometimes he sings yes always the
same song pause SAME SONG yes if he sees things yes
often no little scenes yes in the light yes but not often no as
if a light went on yes as if yes

sky and earth yes people poking about yes all over the place
yes and him there somewhere yes skulking somewhere yes
as if the mud opened yes or turned transparent yes but not
often no not long no otherwise black yes and he calls that
life above yes as against life here pause HERE howls
good

they are not memories no he has no memories no nothing to
prove he was ever above no in the places he sees no but he
may have been yes skulking somewhere yes hugging the
walls yes by night yes he can't affirm anything no deny anything no so one can't speak of memories no but at the same
time one can speak of them yes

if he talks to himself no thinks no believes in God yes every
day no wishes to die yes but doesn't expect to no he ex-
pects to stay where he is yes flat as a cowclap on his belly
yes in the mud yes without motion yes without thought yes
eternally yes

if he is sure of what he says no he can't affirm anything
no he may have forgotten many things no certain lit-

tle things yes the little there was yes such as having crawled a little yes eaten a little yes thought a little murmured a little for himself alone yes heard a human voice no he wouldn't have forgotten that no brushed against a brother before me no he wouldn't have forgotten that no

if he wants me to leave him yes in peace yes without me there is peace yes was peace yes every day no if he thinks I'll leave him no I'll stay where I am yes glued to him yes tormenting him yes eternally yes

but he can't affirm anything no deny anything no things may have been different yes his life here pause YOUR LIFE HERE good and deep in the furrows howls thump face in the mud nose mouth howls good he wins he can't

ABOVE the light goes on little scenes in the mud or memories of scenes past he finds the words for the sake of peace HERE howls this life he can't or can't any more he was able once how it was before the other with the other after the other before me the little there was nearly all like me my life here before Pim with Pim how it was the little there was I've said it I've been able I think so as I hear it and say to make an end with him a warning to me murmur to the mud quick quick soon I won't be able either never any Pim never was never anything of all this little quick then the little that is left add it quick before Bom before he comes to ask me how it was my life here before him the little that is left add it quick how it was after Pim before Bom how it is

quick then end at last of part two how it was with Pim leav-

ing at last only part three and last how it was after Pim
before Bom how it is saying as I hear it that one day all
that every word always as I hear it in me that was without quaqua the voice of us all when the panting stops and
murmur in the mud to the mud that one day come back to
myself to Pim why not known not said from the nothing
come back from the nothing the surprise to find myself
alone at last no more Pim me alone in the dark the mud end
at last of part two how it was with Pim leaving at last only
part three and last how it was after Pim before Bom how it
is that's how it was with Pim

3

here then at last I quote on part three how it was after Pim how it is part three at last and last towards which lighter than air an instant flop fallen so many vows sighs prayers without words ever since the first word I hear it the word how

no more time I say it as I hear it murmur it in the mud I'm sinking sinking fast too strong no more head imagination spent no more breath

the vast past near and far the old today of the extreme old even the humming-bird known as the passing moment all that

the vast past even the humming-bird it comes in from the right I watch it fly lightning semi-circle deasil then respite then the next then then or eyes closed it's preferable head bowed or not before the storm brief blanks good moments brief blacks then zzizz then next all that

all that almost blank that was so adorned a few traces that's all seeing who I always more or less so little so little there but there little there but there no alternative

before Pim long before with Pim vast tracts of time kinds of thoughts same family divers doubts emotions too yes emotions some with tears yes tears motions too and movements both parts and whole as when he sets out to seek out all of him sets out to seek out the true home

there then more or less more of old less of late very little these last tracts they are the last extremely little hardly at all a few seconds on and off enough to mark a life several lives crosses everywhere indelible traces

all that almost blank nothing to get out of it almost nothing
nothing to put in that's the saddest that would be the saddest imagination on the decline having attained the bottom
what one calls sinking one is tempted

or ascending heaven at last no place like it in the end

or not stirring that too that's defendable half in the mud
half out

no more head in any case hardly any no more heart just
enough to be thankful for it a little thankful to be so little
there and sinking a little at last having attained the bottom

a little cheerful the less you're there the more you're cheerful when you're there less tears a little less when you're
there words lacking all lacking less tears for lack of words
lack of food even birth it's lacking all that makes you cheerful it must be that all that a little more cheerful

how it was that's lacking before Pim with Pim all lost almost
all nothing left almost nothing but it's done great blessing
leaving only sithence how it was after Pim how it is vast
stretch of time before Pim with Pim vast tracts of time a few
minutes on and off added up vast stretch eternity same scale
of magnitude nothing there almost nothing

clench the eyes I quote on not the blue the others at the
back see something somewhere after Pim that's all is left
breath in a head nothing left but a head nothing in it al-

most nothing only breath pant pant hundred to the minute
hold it be it held ten seconds fifteen seconds hear something try and hear a few old words after Pim how it was
how it is quick

Pim quick after Pim before he vanishes never was only me
me Pim how it was before me with me after me how it is
quick

a sack bravo colour of mud in the mud quick say a sack
colour of its surroundings having assumed it always had it
it's one or the other seek no further what else that thing
could possibly be so many things say sack old word first
to come one syllable k at the end seek no other all would
vanish a sack that will do the word the thing it's a possible
thing in this world so little possible yes world what more
can you ask a possible thing see it name it name it see it
enough now rest I'll be back no alternative some day

stop panting say what you hear see what you say say you
see it an arm colour of mud the hand in the sack quick say
an arm then another say another arm see it stretched taut
as though too short to reach now add a hand fingers parted
stretched taut monstrous nails all that say you see all
that

a body what matter say a body see a body all the rear white
originally some light spots still say grey of hair growing
still that's enough a head say a head say you've seen a head
all that all the possible a sack with food a body entire alive
still yes living stop panting let it stop ten seconds fifteen
seconds hear this breath token of life hear it said say you
hear it good pant on

[105]

on and off as if borne on the wind but not a breath sharp and faint God's old clapper old mill threshing the void or in another mood as though it changed great shears of the black old hag older than the world born of night click clack click clack two threads a second five every two never mine

no more I'll hear no more see no more yes I must to make an end a few more old words find a few more not quite so old as when Pim part two those are done never were but old too vast stretch of time this voice these voices as if borne on all the winds but not a breath another antiquity a little more recent stop panting let it stop ten seconds fifteen seconds a few old words on and off string them together make phrases

a few old images always the same no more blue the blue is done never was the sack the arms the body the mud the dark living hair and nails all that

my voice no objection back at last a voice back at last in my mouth my mouth no objection a voice at last in the dark the mud unimaginable tracts of time

this breath hold this breath be it held once twice per day and night the time that means to those under whom and all above and all about the earth turns and all turns who hasten so from one goal to the next that but for this breath I would fancy I hear their hastening feet hold it be it held ten seconds fifteen seconds try and hear

of this old tale quaqua on all sides then in me bits and scraps try and hear a few scraps two or three each time per day and night string them together make phrases more phrases the last how it was after Pim how it is something wrong there end of part three and last

this voice these voices no knowing not meaning a choir no no only one but quaqua meaning on all sides megaphones possibly technique something wrong there

wrong for never twice the same unless time vast tracts aged out of recognition no for often fresher stronger after than before unless sickness sorrow they sometimes pass one feels better less wretched after than before

unless recordings on ebonite or suchlike a whole life generations on ebonite one can imagine it nothing to prevent one mix it all up change the natural order play about with that

unless unchanging after all the voice we're talking of the voice and all my fault lack of attention want of memory the various times mixed up in my head all the various times before during after vast tracts of time

and always the same old thing the same old things possible and impossible or me my fault who can find nothing else when the panting stops hear nothing else the same old things four or five a few adornments life above little scenes

things said to me said of me to whom else of whom else clench the eyes try and see another to whom of whom to whom of me of whom to me or even a third clench the eyes try and see a third mix up all that

quaqua the voice of us all who all all those here be-

fore me and to come alone in this wallow or glued together all the Pims tormentors promoted victims past if it
ever passes and to come that's sure more than ever by the
earth undone its light all those

from it I learn from it I learnt what little remained learn
what little remains of how it was before Pim with Pim after
Pim and how it is for that too it found words

for how it would be when I had it no more before I had mine
that vast pit and when I had it at last that vast stretch
how it would be then when I had mine at last and when
I had it no more mine no more how it would be then

the moment when I would need to say and could not mamma
papa hear those sounds slake my thirst for labials and could
not from then on words for that moment and following vast
stretch of time

movements for nothing of the lower face no sound no word
and then not even that no further point no more reliance to
be placed on that when it's the last hope look for something else how it would be then words for that

from it all that of that so little what little remains I've named
myself the panting stops and I am an instant that old ever
dwindling little that I think I hear of an ancient voice
quaqua on all sides the voice of us all as many as we are
as many as we'll end if we ever end by having been something wrong there

namely days of great gaiety thicker than on earth since the
age of gold above in the light the leaves fallen dead

some on the bough flutter on to the reawakening black dead flaunting in the green shit yes some in this condition manage two springs a summer and half three-quarters

before Pim the journey part one right leg right arm push pull ten yards fifteen yards halt nap a sardine or suchlike tongue in the mud an image or two little scenes mute words hang on off again push pull all that part one but before that again

another story leave it dark no the same story not two stories leave it dark all the same like the rest a little darker a few words all the same a few old words like for the rest stop panting let it stop

try and hear a few old words on and off string them together in a phrase a few phrases try and see how it can possibly have been not before Pim that's done part one before that again vast stretch of time

two there were two of us his hand on my arse someone had come Bom Bem one syllable m at the end all that matters Bem had come to cleave to me see later Pim and me I had come to cleave to Pim the same thing except that me Pim Bem me Bem left me south

Bem come to cleave to me where I lay abandoned to give me a name his name to give me a life make me talk of a life said to have been mine above in the light before I fell all the already said part two with Pim another part two before part one except that me Pim Bem me Bem left me south I hear it murmur it in the mud

together then life in common me Bem he Bem we Bem vast
stretch of time until the day hear day say day murmur it
don't be ashamed as if there were an earth a sun moments
of less dark more dark there laugh

dark bright those words each time they come night day
shadow light that family the wish to laugh each time no
sometimes three every ten four every fifteen that ratio try
sometimes same ratio succeed sometimes same ratio

bright dark that family for every hundred times they come
three laughs four laughs brought off the kind that convulse
an instant resurrect an instant then leave for deader than
before

until the day murmur day don't be ashamed when to his
surprise something there Bem alone in the dark the mud
and end for him of that part for me too to my surprise too
something there too as I depart right leg right arm push
pull ten yards fifteen yards towards Pim unwitting long long
journey

time to forget all lose all be ignorant of all whence I come
whither I go frequent halts brief naps a sardine tongue in
the mud loss of the speech so dearly regained a few images
skies homes little scenes falls half out of species brief movements of the lower no sound loss of the noble name of Bem
part one before Pim how it was vast stretch of time it's
done

it's come it's said it's murmured in the mud how it
was not before Pim that's done part one before that
again vast stretch of time very pretty but not right some-

thing wrong something quite wrong

it's the sack Pim left me without his sack he left his sack
with me I left my sack with Bem I'll leave my sack with Bom
I left Bem without my sack to go towards Pim it's the sack

Bem then I was with Bem before going towards Pim I left
Bem then without my sack and yet that sack that I had
going towards Pim part one that sack that I had

that sack then that I did not have on leaving Bem and that
I had going towards Pim not knowing I had left anyone was
going towards anyone that sack then that I had I must have
found it there's reason in me yet that sack without which
no journey

a sack no doing without a sack without food when you journey as we have seen should have seen part one no doing
without them it's regulated thus we're regulated thus

leaving then without a sack I had a sack I had found it on
my way there is that difficulty overcome we leave our sacks
to those who do not need them we take their sacks from
those who soon will need them we leave without a sack we
find one on our way we can continue on our way

a sack that if one died here one might say had belonged to
one dead at last having let it go at the last then sunk beneath
the mud but no and so a simple sack pure and simple a small
coal-sack to the feel five stone six stone wet jute food inside

a simple sack then pure and simple that no sooner on our way without food or thought of ever finding any or memory of ever having had any or notion of ever needing any we find no sooner on our way in the dark the mud for a journey that would otherwise be brief and is not brief vast stretch of time and take unto ourselves and lose a little before arrival together with the uneaten food as we have seen part one how it was before Pim

more sacks here then than souls infinitely if we journey infinitely and what infinite loss without profit there is that difficulty overcome something wrong there

at the instant I leave Bem another leaves Pim and let us be at that instant one hundred thousand strong then fifty thousand departures fifty thousand abandoned no sun no earth nothing turning the same instant always everywhere

at the instant I reach Pim another reaches Bem we are regulated thus our justice wills it thus fifty thousand couples again at the same instant the same everywhere with the same space between them it's mathematical it's our justice in this muck where all is identical our ways and way of faring right leg right arm push pull

as long as I with Pim the other with Bem a hundred thousand prone glued two by two together vast stretch of time nothing stirring save the tormentors those whose turn it is on and off right arm claw the armpit for the song carve the scriptions plunge the opener pestle the kidney all the needful

at the instant Pim leaves me and goes towards the other Bem leaves the other and comes towards me I place myself at my point of view migration of slime-worms then or tailed latrinal scissiparous frenzy days of great gaiety

at the instant Pim reaches the other to form again with him the only couple he forms apart from the one with me Bem reaches me to form with me the only couple he forms apart from the one with the other

illumination here Bem is therefore Bom or Bom Bem and the voice quaqua from which I get my life these scraps of life in me when the panting stops of three things one

when according to me it said Bem speaking of how it was before the journey part one and Bom speaking of how it will be after the abandon part three and last it said in reality

it said in reality in the one case as in the other either Bem solely or solely Bom

or it said in reality now Bem now Bom through carelessness or inadvertence not realizing that it varied I personify it it personifies itself

or finally it passed prepensely from the one to the other according as it spoke of how it was before the journey or of how it will be after the abandon through ignorance not realizing that Bem and Bom could only be one and the same

that it was vain to wish for him an unfamiliar guise whose coming it announced right leg right arm push pull ten yards fifteen yards that he was necessarily that ancient other whom it said I had suffered then forsaken to go towards Pim as Pim me suffered then forsaken to go towards his other

to no unwitting all here unwitting our justice go never from never towards

unwitting that each always leaves the same always goes towards the same always loses the same always goes towards him who leaves him always leaves him who goes towards him our justice

millions millions there are millions of us and there are three I place myself at my point of view Bem is Bom Bom Bem let us say Bom it's preferable Bom then me and Pim me in the middle

so in me I quote on when the panting stops scraps of that ancient voice on itself its errors and exactitudes on us millions on us three our couples journeys and abandons on me alone I quote on my imaginary journeys imaginary brothers in me when the panting stops that was without quaqua on all sides bits and scraps I murmur them

a voice which if I had a voice I might have taken for mine which at the instant I hear it I quote on is also heard by him whom Bom left to come towards me and by him to go towards whom Pim left me and if we are a million strong by the other 499997 abandoned

the same voice the same things nothing changing but the names and hardly they two are enough nameless each awaits his Bom nameless goes towards his Pim

[114]

Bom to the abandoned not me Bom you Bom we Bom but me Bom you Pim I to the abandoned not me Pim you Pim we Pim but me Bom you Pim something very wrong there

so eternally I quote on something lost there so eternally now Bom now Pim something wrong there according as left or right north or south tormentor or victim these words too strong tormentor always of the same and victim always of the same and now alone journeying abandoned all alone nameless all these words too strong almost all a little too strong I say it as I hear it

or one alone one name alone the noble name of Pim and I hear wrong or the voice says wrong and when I hear Bom or it says Bom in me when the panting stops the scrap Bom that was without quaqua on all sides

when I hear or in fact it says that before going towards Pim part one I was with Bom as Pim with me part two

and that at this moment part three right leg right arm push pull Bom towards me as I towards Pim part one

it's Pim that should be heard Pim that should have been said that I was with Pim before going towards Pim part one and that at this moment part three Pim towards me as I towards Pim part one right leg right arm push pull ten yards fifteen yards

a million then if a million strong a million Pims now motion-less agglutinated two by two in the interests of torment too strong five hundred thousand little heaps colour of mud and now a thousand thousand nameless solitaries half abandoned half abandoning

and three if three when in me the panting stops this voice
which was without quaqua on all sides when I hear it speak
of millions and of three which if I had a voice I quote a
little heart a little head I might take for mine then I alone
hear it who alone am abandoned

alone murmur of millions and of three our journeys couples
and abandons and the name we give to one another and
give and give again

alone hear these scraps and murmur them in the mud to the
mud my two companions as we have seen being on their
way he who is coming towards me and he who is going from
me something wrong there that is to say each in his part
one

or in his part five or nine or thirteen so on

correct

whereas the voice as we have seen peculiar to part three
or seven or eleven or fifteen so on just as the couple to part
two or four or six or eight so on

correct

assuming one prefers the order here proposed namely one
the journey two the couple three the abandon to that to
those to be obtained by starting with the abandon and ending with the journey by way of the couple or by starting
with the couple and ending with the

with the couple

by way of the abandon

or of the journey

correct

something wrong there

and if on the contrary I alone then no further problem a
solution which without a serious effort of the imagination
it would seem difficult to avoid

as for example our course a closed curve and let us be
numbered 1 to 1000000 then number 1000000 on leaving his
tormentor number 999999 instead of launching forth into
the wilderness towards an inexistent victim proceeds towards number 1

and number 1 forsaken by his victim number 2 does not remain eternally bereft of tormentor since this latter as we
have seen in the person of number 1000000 is approaching
with all the speed he can muster right leg right arm push
pull ten yards fifteen yards

and three if only three of us and so numbered only 1 to 3
four rather it's preferable clearer picture if only four of us
and so numbered only 1 to 4

then two places only at the extremities of the greatest chord
say A and B for the four couples the four abandoned

two tracks only of a semi-orbit each say how shall we say AB and BA for the travellers

let me for example be numbered 1 it's not asking a great deal and at a given moment find myself abandoned that is to say again abandoned at the extremity A of the great chord and assuming we turn deasil

then before I can find myself again at the same point and in much the same state I shall have been successively

victim of number 4 at A en route along AB tormentor of number 2 at B abandoned again but this time at B victim again of number 4 but this time at B en route again but this time along BA tormentor of number 2 again but this time at A and finally abandoned again at A and all set to begin again

correct

for each one of us then if only four of us before the initial situation can be restored two abandons two journeys four couplings of which two on the left or north tormenting always the same in my case number 2 and two on the right or south tormented always by the same in my case number 4

as for number 3 I do not know him nor consequently he me just as number 2 and number 4 do not know each other

for each of us then if only four of us one of us for ever unknown or known only by repute there is that possibility

I frequent number 4 and number 2 in my quality of victim and tormentor respectively and number 2 and number 4 frequent number 3 in their quality of tormentor and victim respectively

possible then in principle that to number 3 on the one hand through my victim whose victim he is and on the other through my tormentor whose tormentor he is possible then I repeat I quote in principle that to number 3 I am not a total stranger without our ever having occasion to meet

similarly if a million strong each knows personally only his tormentor and victim in other words him who comes immediately behind him and him who goes immediately before him

and by them alone is personally known

but may quite conceivably in principle know by repute the 999997 others whom by virtue of his position in the round he has never occasion to meet

and by repute by them be known

for take twenty consecutive numbers

no matter which no matter which it is irrelevant

814326 to 814345

number 814327 may speak misnomer the tormentors being mute as we have seen part two may speak of number 814326 to number 814328 who may speak of him to number 814329 who may speak of him to number 814330 and so on to num-

ber 814345 who in this way may know number 814326 by
repute

similarly number 814326 may know by repute number
814345 number 814344 having spoken of him to number
814343 and this last to number 814342 and this last to number 814341 and so back to number 814326 who in this way
may know number 814345 by repute

rumour transmissible ad infinitum in either direction

from left to right through the confidences of the tormentor
to his victim who repeats them to his

from right to left through the confidences of the victim to
his tormentor who repeats them to his

all these words I repeat I quote on victims tormentors confidences repeat quote I and the others all these words too
strong I say it again as I hear it again murmur it again to the
mud infinitum alone commensurate with us

but question to what purpose

for when number 814336 describes number 814337 to number 814335 and number 814335 to number 814337 for example he is merely in fact describing himself to two lifelong
acquaintances

so to what purpose

moreover the thing would appear to be impossible

for number 814336 as we have seen by the time he reaches number 814337 has long since forgotten all he ever knew of number 814335 as completely as though he had never been and by the time number 814335 reaches him as we have also seen has long since forgotten all he ever knew of number 814337 vast stretch of time

so true it is that here one knows one's tormentor only as long as it takes to suffer him and one's victim only as long as it takes to enjoy him if as long

and these same couples that eternally form and form again all along this immense circuit that the millionth time that's conceivable is as the inconceivable first and always two strangers uniting in the interests of torment

and when on the unpredictable arse for the millionth time the groping hand descends that for the hand it is the first arse for the arse the first hand

something wrong there

so true the panting stops I hear it I murmur it to the mud so true all that is

so no acquaintance by hearsay and as for the other or personal acquired by frequentation that which with his tormentor on the one hand with his victim on the other each one of us may boast as for it

when you think of the couple we were Pim and I part two and shall be again part six ten fourteen so on each time for the unthinkable first when you think of that what we were then each for himself and for the other

glued together like a single body in the dark the mud

how at each instant each ceased and was there no more either for himself or for the other vast tracts of time

and when we came back to be together for an instant again when you think of that

cruelty suffering so paltry and brief

the paltry need of a life a voice of one who has neither

the voice extorted a few words life because of cry that's the proof good and deep no more is needed a little cry all is not dead one drinks one gives to drink goodbye

they were I quote good moments somehow or other good moments when you think

Pim and me part two and Bom and me part four what that will be

to say after that that we knew each other personally even then

glued together like a single body in the dark the mud

motionless but for one right arm brief flurry on and of all the needful to say after that that I knew Pim that Pim knew me and Bom and I that we shall know each other even fleetingly

you may say yes and you may say no it depends on what you hear

it's no I'm sorry no one here knows anyone either personally or otherwise it's the no that turns up I murmur it

and no again I'm sorry again no one here knows himself it's the place without knowledge whence no doubt its peerlessness

whether four then revolving or a million four strangers a million strangers to themselves to one another but here I quote on we do not revolve

that is above in the light where their space is measured here the straight line the straight line eastward strange and death in the west as a rule

so neither four nor a million

nor ten million nor twenty million nor any finite number even or uneven however great because of our justice which wills that not one were we fifty million not a single one among us be wronged

not one deprived of tormentor as number 1 would be not one deprived of victim as number 50000000 would be assuming this latter at the head of the procession which wends as we have seen from left to right or if you prefer from west to east and that there be never offered to the eyes of

of whom

of him in charge of the sacks

possible

to his eyes the spectacle on the one hand of a single one among us towards whom no one ever goes and on the other of a single other who never goes towards anyone it would be an injustice and that is above in the light

in other words in simple words I quote on either I am alone and no further problem or else we are innumerable and no further problem either

save that of conceiving but no doubt it can be done a procession in a straight line with neither head nor tail in the dark the mud with all the various infinitudes that such a conception involves

nothing to be done in any case we have our being in justice I have never heard anything to the contrary

with that of a slowness difficult to conceive the procession we are talking of a procession advancing in jerks or spasms like shit in the guts till one wonders days of great gaiety if we shall not end one after another or two by two by being shat into the open air the light of day the regimen of grace

a slowness of which figures alone however arbitrary can give a feeble idea allowing then I quote twenty years for the journey and knowing furthermore from having heard so that the four phases through which we pass the two kinds of solitude the two kinds of company through which tormentors abandoned victims travellers we all pass and pass again being regulated thus are of equal duration

knowing furthermore by the same courtesy that the journey is accomplished in stages ten yards fifteen yards at the rate of say it's reasonable to say one stage per month this word these words months years I murmur them

four by twenty eighty twelve and half by twelve one hundred and fifty by twenty three thousand divided by eighty thirty-seven and a half thirty-seven to thirty-eight say forty yards a year we advance

correct

from left to right we advance each one advances and all advance from west to east year in year out in the dark the mud in torment and solitude at the speed of thirty-seven to thirty-eight say forty yards a year we advance

such the feeble idea of our slowness given by these figures of which it is sufficient to admit and no doubt it can be done on the one hand that assigned to the duration of the journey and on the other those expressing the length and frequency of the stage to obtain this feeble idea of our slowness

our slowness the slowness of our procession from left to right in the dark the mud an image in its discontinuity of the journeys of which it is the sum made up of stages and of halts and of those stages of which the journey is the sum

when we crawl in an amble right leg right arm push pull flat on face mute maledictions left leg left arm push pull flat on face mute maledictions ten yards fifteen yards halt

all that once without quaqua on all sides now in me when the panting stops all that fainter weaker but still audible less clear but the purport in me when the panting stops

and that here in truth all discontinuous journey images torment even solitude part three when a voice speaks then stops a few scraps then nothing more save the dark the mud all discontinuous save the dark the mud

an image too of this voice ten words fifteen words long silence ten words fifteen words long silence long solitude once without quaqua on all sides vast stretch of time then in me when the panting stops scraps

from it everything I know how it was before Pim before that again with Pim after Pim how it is words for that too how it will be words for that in a word my life vast tracts of time

I hear me again murmur me in the mud and am again

the journey I made in the dark the mud straight line sack tied to my neck never quite fallen from my species and I made that journey then something else and I didn't make it then again and I made it again

and Pim how I found him made him suffer made him speak and lost him and all that while it lasts I had it all when the panting stops

and how there are three of us four a million and there I am always was with Pim Bom and another and 999997 others journeying alone rotting alone martyring and being martyred oh moderately listlessly a little blood a few cries life above in the light a little blue little scenes for the thirst for the sake of peace

and how there cannot be only three of us only four only a million and there I am always was with Pim Bom innumerable others in a procession without end or beginning languidly wending from left to right straight line eastward strange in the dark the mud sandwiched between victim and tormentor and how these words not weak enough most of them not quite enough

or alone and no further problem never any Pim never any Bom never any journey never anything but the dark the mud the sack perhaps too it seems constant too and this voice which knows not what it says or I hear wrong which if I had a voice a little heart a little head I might take for mine once without quaqua on all sides then in me when the panting stops faint now scarce a breath

all that all that while it lasts all those kinds of lives when the panting stops I had it all it depends on what you hear knew it all did and suffered as the case may be in the present too and in the future that's sure a matter of hearing nothing more when the panting stops ten seconds fifteen seconds all those kinds of lives bits and scraps murmur them to the mud

and finally how now the panting wilder more and more animal in want of air and to stop it again for it to stop again so wild a panting and this voice to hear it again that was without quaqua on all sides now in me when the panting stops how that will soon no doubt be possible no more

at that moment I quote on from that moment on and following I being this voice these scraps nothing more shall at last be no more but without ceasing for such a trifle end of part three and last it must be almost ended

that yes a panting in the mud to that it all comes in the end the journey the couple the abandon when the whole tale is told the tormentor you are said to have had then lost the journey you are said to have made the victim you are said to have had then lost the images the sack the little fables of above little scenes a little blue infernal homes

the voice quaqua on all sides then within in the little vault empty closed eight planes bone-white if there were a light a tiny flame all would be white ten words fifteen words like a fume of sighs when the panting stops then the storm the breath token of life part three and last it must be nearly ended

then that you have your life and that you had it the long journeys and company of your likes lost and forsaken when the panting stops to that it all comes in the end a pant-

ing in the dark the mud not unlike certain laughs but
not one

or then that all begins and then the life you'll have the tormentor you'll have the journey you'll make the victim
you'll have the two lives the three lives the life you had the
life you have the life you'll have

hard to conceive this last when instead of beginning as
traveller I begin as victim and instead of continuing as tormentor I continue as traveller and instead of ending abandoned

instead of ending abandoned I end as tormentor

the essential would seem to be lacking

this solitude when the voice recounts it sole means of living
it

my life we're talking of my life

unless it recounts it the voice my life during that other solitude when I journey that is to say instead of a first past a
second past and a present a past a present and a future
something wrong there

refreshing alternations of history prophesy and latest news
whereby I learn in turn it's no doubt what keeps me young
how it was my life we're still talking of my life

how it was before Pim how it was with Pim how it is present
formulation

how it was with Bom how it is how it will be with Pim

how it is how it will be with Bom how it will be before Pim

how it was my life still with Pim how it is how it will be with Bom

fleeting impression I quote that in trying to present in three parts or episodes an affair which all things considered involves four one is in danger of being incomplete

that to this third part now ending at last a fourth should normally be appended in which would be seen among a thousand and one other things scarcely or not at all to be seen in the present formulation this thing

instead of me sticking the opener into Pim's arse Bom sticking it into mine

and instead of Pim's cries his song and exorted voice be heard indistinguishably similar mine

but we shall never see Bom at work I shall pant on in abeyance in the dark the mud the voice being so ordered I quote that of our total life it states only three quarters

now the first second and third now the fourth first and second

now the third fourth and first now the second third and fourth something wrong there

and so ordered that it is loath for the episode couple even in its twofold aspect to figure twice in the same communication as would be the case if instead of having me begin as traveller present formulation or as abandoned possible formulation it had me begin as tormentor or as victim

need then to emend what has just been said in which it succeeds by saying in its stead that of the four three quarters of our total life only three lend themselves to communication

the three quarters of which the first the journey present formulation and the three quarters of which the first the abandon formulation equally defendable

loathing most understandable if it be kindly considered that the two solitudes that of the journey and that of the abandon differ appreciably and consequently merit separate treatment whereas the two couples that in which I figure in the north as tormentor and that in which I figure in the south as victim compose the same spectacle exactly

having already appeared with Pim in my quality of tormentor part two I have not to take cognizance of a part four in which I would appear with Bom in my quality of victim it is sufficient for this episode to be announced Bom comes right leg right arm push pull ten yards fifteen yards

or emotions sensations take a sudden interest in them and even then what the fuck I quote does it matter who suffers faint waver here faint tremor the fuck who suffers who makes to suffer who cries who to be left in peace in the dark the mud gibbers ten seconds fifteen seconds of sun clouds earth sea patches of blue clear nights and of a creature if not still standing still capable of standing always the same imagination spent looking for a hole that he may be seen no more in the middle of this faery who drinks that drop of piss of being and who with his last gasp pisses it to drink the moment it's someone each in his turn as our justice wills and never any end it wills that too all dead or none

two possible formulations therefore the present and that other beginning where the present ends and consequently ending with the journey in the dark the mud the traveller right leg right arm push pull coming so utterly from nowhere and no one and so utterly on his way there that he has never ceased from travelling will never cease from travelling dragging his sack where provisions are dwindling but not so fast as appetite

that cognizance then of the present communication be taken backward and once studied from left to right its course be retraced from right to left no objection

on condition that by an effort of the imagination the still central episode of the couple be duly adjusted

all that once without scraps in me when the panting stops ten seconds fifteen seconds all that fainter weaker less clear but the purport in me when it abates the breath we're talking of a breath token of life when it abates like a last in the light then resumes a hundred and ten fifteen to the minute when it abates ten seconds fifteen seconds

it's then I hear it my life here a life somewhere said to have
been mine still mine and still in store bits and scraps
strung together vast stretch of time an old tale my old
life each time Pim leaves me till Bom finds me it is
there

words quaqua then in me when the panting stops bits and
scraps a murmur this old life same old words same old
scraps millions of times each time the first how it was before
Pim before that again with Pim after Pim before Bom how
it is how it will be all that words for all that in me I hear
them murmur them

my life ten seconds fifteen seconds it's then I have it murmur it it's preferable more logical brief movements of the
lower face with murmur in the mud

of an ancient voice ill-spoken ill-heard murmur ill some ancient scraps for Kram who listens Krim who notes or Kram
alone one is enough Kram alone witness and scribe his
lamps their light upon me Kram with me bending over me
till the age-limit then his son his son's son so on

with me when I journey with me with Pim with me abandoned part three and last with me with Bom from age to age
their lamps their light upon me

their books where all is noted whatever little there is to
note my doings my murmur ten seconds fifteen seconds part
three and last present formulation

my life a voice without quaqua on all sides words scraps
then nothing then again more words more scraps the same
ill-spoken ill-heard then nothing vast stretch of time then
in me in the vault bone-white if there were a light bits and
scraps ten seconds fifteen seconds ill-heard ill-murmured
ill-heard ill-recorded my whole life a gibberish garbled six-
fold

the panting stops I hear it my life I have it murmur it it's
preferable more logical for Kram to note and if we are innumerable then Krams innumerable if you like or one alone
my Kram mine alone he's enough here where justice reigns
one life all life not two lives our justice one Kram not one of
us there's reason in me yet his son begets his son leaves the
light Kram goes back up into the light to end his days

or no Kram that too when the panting stops an ear above
somewhere above and unto it the murmur ascending and if
we are innumerable then murmurs innumerable all alike
our justice one life everywhere ill-told ill-heard quaqua on
all sides then within when the panting stops ten seconds
fifteen seconds in the little chamber all bone-white if there
were a light oakum of old words ill-heard ill-murmured
that murmur those murmurs

fallen in the mud from our mouths innumerable and ascending to where there is an ear a mind to understand a means of
noting a care for us the wish to note the curiosity to understand an ear to hear even ill these scraps of other scraps of
an antique rigmarole

immemorial imperishable like us the ear we're talking of an ear above in the light and in that case for us days of great gaiety in that untiring listening to this unchanging drone the faint sign for us of a change some day nay even of an end in all honour and justice

or for which as for us each time the first and in that case no problem

or of the fragile kind made for the blackbirds when to the day the long night yields at last and to the night a little later the interminable day but us this life how it was how it is how most certainly it will be not made for that a second time next per shaving and in that case no surprise to be expected either

all that among other things so many others ill-spoken ill-heard ill-remembered to the sole end that there may be white on white trace of so many and so many words ill-given ill-received ill-rendered to the mud and whose ear in these conditions the gift of understanding the care for us the means of noting what does it matter

whose his in charge of the sacks the sacks possible and food these words again the sack as we have seen

the sack as we have seen there being occasions when the sack as we have seen is more than a mere larder for us yes moments when if needs be it may appear more than a mere larder to us

those words of old in their place of old end of part three and last present formulation at the end before the si-

lence the panting without pause the animal in want of air
the mouth murmuring them to the mud and the continu-
ation of old when the panting stops ten words fifteen words
a murmur to the mud

and later much later these aeons my God when it stops again
ten more fifteen more in me a murmur scarce a breath then
from mouth to mud brief kiss brush of lips faint kiss

namely string them together last reasonings namely these
sacks these sacks one must understand try and understand
these sacks innumerable with us here for our journeys innumerable on this narrow track one foot two foot all here in
position already like us all here in position at the inconceivable start of this caravan no impossible

impossible that at at every journey we should have had to
scale a mountain of sacks and should still have and should
for ever have each one of us at every journey in order to
reach his victim to scale a mountain of sacks our progress
as we have seen while admittedly laborious yet the terrain
the terrain try and understand no accidents no asperities our
justice

last reasonings last figures number 777777 leaves number
777776 on his way unwitting towards number 777778 finds
the sack without which he would not go far takes it unto
himself and continues on his way the same to be taken
by number 777776 in his turn and after him by number
777775 and so back to the unimaginable number 1 each one
no sooner on his way than he finds the sack indispensable to
his journey and not to be relinquished till a little before
arrival as we have seen

whence if all the sacks in position like us at the beginning that hypothesis such an acervation of sacks on the track nay concentrated in a little room since each finds his as we have seen his sack we are talking of our sacks no sooner his tormentor forsaken as he must if he is ever to reach his victim as we have seen if his victim is ever to be reached

such an acervation of sacks at the very outset that all progress impossible and no sooner imparted to the caravan the unthinkable first impulsion than arrested for ever and frozen in injustice

then from left to right or west to east the atrocious spectacle on into the black night of boundless futurity of the abandoned tormentor never to be victim then a little space then his brief journey done prostrate at the foot of a mountain of provisions the victim never to be tormentor then a great space then another abandoned so on infinitely

for clear as day that similarly obstructed without exception each and every section of track or segment between consecutive couples consecutive abandons according as one considers it the track we're talking of the track its sections or segments before the departures or during the journeys the panting stops and clear as day that similarly obstructed without exception each and every section or segment and for the same reasons our justice

thus need for the billionth time part three and last present formulation at the end before the silence the panting without pause if we are to be possible our couplings journeys and abandons need of one not one of us an intelligence somewhere a love who all along the track at the right places according as we need them deposits our sacks

ten yards fifteen yards to the east of the couples the abandoned according as deposited before the departures or during the journeys those are the right places

and to whom given our number not unreasonable to attribute exceptional powers or else at his beck assistants innumerable and to whom in pursuance of the principle of parsimony not excessive at times ten seconds fifteen seconds to assign the ear which Kram eliminated our murmur demands otherwise desert flower

and that minimum of intelligence without which it were an ear like ours and that strange care for us not to be found among us and the wish and ability to note which we have not

cumulation of offices most understandable if it will be kindly considered that to hear and note one of our murmurs is to hear and note them all

and sudden light on the sacks at what moment renewed at some moment in the life of the couples since it is while the victim journeys as we have seen and indeed see that the abandoned tormentor murmurs or else ring the knell while following the hearse it's possible too there's a poor light

and to whom at times not extravagant to impute that voice quaqua the voice of us all of which now when the panting stops ten seconds fifteen seconds definitely the last scraps to have come down to us and in what a state there he is then at last that not one of us there we are then at last who listens to himself and who when he lends his ear to our murmur does no more than lend it to a story of his own devising ill-inspired ill-told and so ancient so forgotten at each telling that ours may seem faithful that we murmur to the mud to him

and this life in the dark and mud its joys and sorrows journeys intimacies and abandons as with a single voice perpetually broken now one half of us and now the other we exhale it pretty much the same as the one he had devised

and of which untiringly every twenty or forty years according to certain of our figures he recalls to our abandoned the essential features

and this anonymous voice self-styled quaqua the voice of us all that was without on all sides then in us when the panting stops bits and scraps barely audible certainly distorted there it is at last the voice of him who before listening to us murmur what we are tells us what we are as best he can

of him to whom we are further indebted for our unfailing rations which inable us to advance without pause or rest

of him who God knows who could blame him must sometimes wonder if to these perpetual revictuallings narrations and auditions he might not put an end without ceasing to maintain us in some kind of being without end and some kind of justice without flaw who could blame him and if finally he might not with profit revise us by means for example of a pronouncement to the effect that this diversity is not our portion nor these refreshing transitions from solitary travellers to tormentors of our immediate fellows and from abandoned tormentors to their victims

nor all this black air that breathes through our ranks and enshrines as in a thebaïd our couples and our solitudes as well of the journey as of the abandon

but that in reality we are one and all from the unthinkable first to the no less unthinkable last glued together in a vast imbrication of flesh without breach or fissure

for as we have seen part two how it was with Pim the coming into contact of mouth and ear leads to a slight overlapping of flesh in the region of the shoulders

and that linked thus bodily together each one of us is at the same time Bom and Pim tormentor and tormented pedant and dunce wooer and wooed speechless and reafflicted with speech in the dark the mud nothing to emend there

there he is then again last figures the inevitable number 777777 at the instant when he buries the opener in the arse of number 777778 and is rewarded by a feeble cry cut short as we have seen by the thump on skull who on being stimulated at the same instant and in the same way by number 777776 makes his own private moan which same fate

something wrong there

and who at the instant when clawed in the armpit by number 777776 he sings applies the same treatment to number 777778 with no less success

so on and similarly all along the chain in both directions for all our other joys and sorrows all we extort and endure from one another from the one to the other inconceivable end of this immeasurable wallow

formulation to be adjusted assuredly in the light of our limits and possibilities but which will always present this advantage that by eliminating all journeys all abandons it eliminates at the same stroke all occasion of sacks and voices quaqua then in us when the panting stops

and the procession which seemed as if it must be eternal our justice the advantage of stopping it without prejudice to a single one among us for try and stop it without first closing our ranks and of two things one

it is stopped at the season of our couples and in that case one half of us tormentors in perpetuity victims in perpetuity the other

it is stopped at the season of our journeys and in that case solitude guaranteed for all assuredly but not in justice since the traveller to whom life owes a victim will never have another and never another tormentor the abandoned to whom life owes one

and other iniquities leave them dark pant wilder one is enough last scraps very last when the panting stops try and catch them last murmurs very last namely first to have done with this not one of us

his dream of putting an end to our journeys abandons need of sustenance and murmurs

to the extenuating purveyances of every description that devolve on him in consequence

without being reduced on that account to whelming us one and all even to the unimaginable last at one stroke in this black mud and nothing on its surface ever more to sully it

in justice and the safeguard of our essential activities

this new formulation namely this new life to have done with that

sudden question if in spite of this conglomeration of all our bodies we are not still the object of a slow translation from west to east one is tempted

if it will kindly be considered that while it is in our interest as tormentors to remain where we are as victims our urge is to move on

and that of these two aspirations warring in each heart it would be normal for the latter to triumph if only narrowly

for as we have seen in the days that word again of journeys and abandons a most remarkable thing when you come to think of it only the victims journeyed

the tormentors as though struck numb with stupor instead
of giving chase right leg right arm push pull ten yards fifteen yards lying where abandoned penalty perhaps of their
recent exertions but effect also of our justice

though in what this diminished by a general free for all one
does not see

involving for one and all the same obligation precisely
that of fleeing without fear while pursuing without
hope

and if it is still possible at this late hour to conceive of other
worlds

as just as ours but less exquisitely organized

one perhaps there is one perhaps somewhere merciful
enough to shelter such frolics where no one ever abandons
anyone and no one ever waits for anyone and never two
bodies touch

and if it may seem strange that without food to sustain us
we can drag ourselves thus by the mere grace of our united
net sufferings from west to east towards an inexistent peace
we are invited kindly to consider

that for the likes of us and no matter how we are recounted
there is more nourishment in a cry nay a sigh torn from one
whose only good is silence or in speech extorted from
one at last delivered from its use than sardines can ever
offer

to have done then at last with all that last scraps very last
when the panting stops and this voice to have done with this
voice namely this life

this not one of us harping harping mad too with weariness
to have done with him

has he not staring him in the face I quote on a solution more
simple by far and by far more radical

a formulation that would eliminate him completely and so
admit him to that peace at least while rendering me in the
same breath sole responsible for this unqualifiable murmur
of which consequently here the last scraps at last very
last

in the familiar form of questions I am said to ask myself
and answers I am said to give myself however unlikely that
may appear last scraps very last when the panting stops last
murmurs very last however unlikely that may appear

if all that all that yes if all that is not how shall I say no
answer if all that is not false yes

all these calculations yes explanations yes the whole story
from beginning to end yes completely false yes

that wasn't how it was no not at all no how then no answer
how was it then no answer HOW WAS IT screams good

there was something yes but nothing of all that no all balls
from start to finish yes this voice quaqua yes all balls yes on-

ly one voice here yes mine yes when the panting stops
yes

when the panting stops yes so that was true yes the panting
yes the murmur yes in the dark yes in the mud yes to the
mud yes

hard to believe too yes that I have a voice yes in me yes
when the panting stops yes not at other times no and that
I murmur yes I yes in the dark yes in the mud yes for
nothing yes I yes but it must be believed yes

and the mud yes the dark yes the mud and the dark are true
yes nothing to regret there no

but all this business of voices yes quaqua yes of other
worlds yes of someone in another world yes whose kind of
dream I am yes said to be yes that he dreams all the time
yes tells all the time yes his only dream yes his only story
yes

all this business of sacks deposited yes at the end of a cord
no doubt yes of an ear listening to me yes a care for me yes
an ability to note yes all that all balls yes Krim and Kram
yes all balls yes

and all this business of above yes light yes skies yes a little
blue yes a little white yes the earth turning yes bright and
less bright yes little scenes yes all balls yes the women yes
the dog yes the prayers yes the homes yes all balls yes

and this business of a procession no answer this business of a procession yes never any procession no nor any journey no never any Pim no nor any Bom no never anyone no only me no answer only me yes so that was true yes it was true about me yes and what's my name no answer WHAT'S MY NAME screams good

only me in any case yes alone yes in the mud yes the dark yes that holds yes the mud and the dark hold yes nothing to regret there no with my sack no I beg your pardon no no sack either no not even a sack with me no

only me yes alone yes with my voice yes my murmur yes when the panting stops yes all that holds yes panting yes worse and worse no answer WORSE AND WORSE yes flat on my belly yes in the mud yes the dark yes nothing to emend there no the arms spread yes like a cross no answer LIKE A CROSS no answer YES OR NO yes

never crawled no in an amble no right leg right arm push pull ten yards fifteen yards no never stirred no never made to suffer no never suffered no answer NEVER SUFFERED no never abandoned no never was abandoned no so that's life here no answer THAT'S MY LIFE HERE screams good

alone in the mud yes the dark yes sure yes panting yes someone hears me no no one hears me no murmuring sometimes yes when the panting stops yes not at other times no in the mud yes to the mud yes my voice yes mine yes not another's no mine alone yes sure yes when the panting stops yes on and off yes a few words yes a few scraps yes that no one hears no but less and less no answer LESS AND LESS yes

so things may change no answer end no answer I may choke
no answer sink no answer sully the mud no more no answer
the dark no answer trouble the peace no more no answer the
silence no answer die no answer DIE screams I MAY DIE
screams I SHALL DIE screams good

good good end at last of part three and last that's how it
was end of quotation after Pim how it is